Back in the den, Nick settled himself on the sofa and Celeste sat herself gingerly next to him. Boy-made snacks, a movie—this felt like a date. She shook her head violently. No. It did not feel like a date, because she wasn't with Travis—her boyfriend—the boy she went on dates with.

"What's the matter with you?" Nick asked, chewing.

"Nothing, I'm fine," she said quickly. Nick started the movie again and she gazed blankly at the screen. She was going to have to be more discreet about her internal battles. Because it was starting to seem like she was the one who needed help keeping this relationship professional.

## Books by Hailey Abbott:

*Getting Lost with Boys*
*The Secrets of Boys*
*The Perfect Boy*
*Waking Up to Boys*
*Forbidden Boy*
*The Other Boy*
*Boy Crazy*
*Summer Boys*
*Next Summer: A Summer Boys Novel*
*After Summer: A Summer Boys Novel*
*Last Summer: A Summer Boys Novel*
*Summer Girls*
*The Bridesmaid*

# FLIRTING WITH BOYS

◆ ◆ ◆

*Hailey*
ABBOTT

**HARPER** TEEN
*An Imprint of* HarperCollins*Publishers*

alloyentertainment

Produced by Alloy Entertainment
151 West 26th Street, New York, NY 10001

Library of Congress catalog card number: 2008942550
ISBN: 978-0-06-125384-3

Typography by Elizabeth Dresner
09 10 11 12 13   CG/RRDH   10 9 8 7 6 5 4 3 2 1
♦
First Edition

# FLIRTING WITH BOYS

# Chapter One

✦

O h my God!"
Celeste Tippen's best friend almost sent her flying
onto the last row of white folding chairs set up on
Longbrook High School's lawn. Under the hot Palm
Springs sun, dressed-up families were filling the aisles,
clutching graduation programs, and claiming rows of
seats by laying jackets and purses across them. Several
audience members turned to look at the crazy girls in
the back, but Devon Wright didn't let go of Celeste's
elbow.

"What?" Celeste spun around, rubbing her tan arm
where Devon's nails had dug in. That was definitely
going to bruise.

*"Stefan Napoli!"* Devon hissed, frantically smoothing

1

her sleek, shoulder-length black hair behind her ears. "How's my hair?"

Celeste rolled her eyes. "Fabulous, of course. When does your hair ever *not* look perfect?" Devon was now using Celeste's sunglasses as a mirror to apply fuchsia lipstick from an ornate gold tube. Celeste stared at the color. "Wow, that's bright. Are you worried Stefan might not be able see you in this crowd?"

"Hold still." Devon was concentrating on her lower lip. "At least it's *interesting*, Ms. Cherry Chapstick."

"Hey! I like my Chapstick. It goes with everything, it's not expensive—"

"It's nice and safe and boring," Devon finished for her. "I know, it's perfect for you. If you weren't dating Travis, I'd already have held a funeral for your wild side." She clicked the lipstick closed and stuck it in her lime green Prada clutch.

Celeste smiled as she thought of Travis Helding, her boyfriend of almost a year. "Maybe that's why we're so good together. He loosens me up and I bring him down to earth." She turned away and squinted at the figures packed into the rows of chairs in front of them, trying not to wobble in her new black espadrilles. "So, which one is the infamous Stefan?"

"Which *one*?" Devon sounded as if Celeste had asked which one was Justin Timberlake. "Him, obviously." She pointed to a tall guy with tousled brown hair lounging across two seats halfway down toward the stage, his legs sticking out into the aisle.

"Isn't he that guy you were talking to at Logan's party? I think his brother's graduating today," Celeste replied over her shoulder as she searched for seats. "Ugh, why is it so hot?" She lifted her long, wavy chestnut hair off the back of her neck and wondered what stroke of insanity had convinced her to wear her new black D&G sundress to spend hours sitting in the sun at the seniors' graduation.

"Um, I don't know," Devon replied. "Maybe because we live in the middle of the *desert*?"

"Ah, yes. That might be it." Celeste pushed past a group of leggings-clad junior high girls blocking the aisle. "By the way, thanks for coming with me. I don't think I could sit through this ceremony alone without collapsing from boredom."

"Of course. Now when you collapse from boredom, I'll be here to catch you," Devon said. "Kevin Fraser's after-party will be worth sitting through this." She wiggled her eyebrows suggestively and looked up toward the stage. "Hey, where's Travis?"

"Probably back there somewhere." Celeste pointed to the screen hiding the graduating seniors. Black mortarboards bobbed above the top. Celeste was surprised she couldn't pick out Travis's cap in the crowd—her boyfriend was six foot six, a good four inches taller than anyone else in the senior class. Either he was late or had decided that the final moments before his high school graduation would be the perfect time for an outdoor nap. Neither option would be out of character.

"Here." Celeste gave Devon a little shove. "There're two seats together."

The girls settled themselves in the third row from the back. They were surrounded on all sides by moms in Lilly Pulitzer print dresses, dads fumbling with digital cameras, and grandmothers clutching ridiculously large handbags. In front of the sleek stucco archway that marked the school's entrance, a temporary stage had been set up on risers, with folding chairs lining the back and giant potted ferns on either end. A podium was set up just below, while a huge printed banner reading CONGRATULATIONS, LONGBROOK HIGH SCHOOL SENIOR CLASS hung over the whole scene. Celeste could just barely see the atrium of the indoor swimming pool gleaming over the school's red-tile roof.

"Are your parents here?" Devon asked. Celeste jumped slightly.

"My parents?" She whipped her head around. "Where?" Her dad wasn't Travis's biggest fan. The fact that the first time he'd met Travis, Celeste had been only partially clothed and Travis had been only partially sober had a lot to do with that. And nothing in the last eight months had really changed her dad's first impression of her boyfriend, despite Celeste's pleas for him to give Travis a chance. At this point, the farther the two of them stayed apart, the better.

Devon gave her friend a pitying smile and smoothed her purple and pink Cavalli hippie dress over her knees. "You have got to relax, babe. I said, *are* your parents here?"

"Oh." Celeste reclined back into her seat. "No, they didn't come. They're really busy getting ready for the season—you know how that goes." Celeste's parents owned one of the most luxurious, exclusive resorts in Palm Springs. Pinyon Ranch wasn't huge. In fact, it only had twenty guest rooms and a dozen private villas, but it was known for its five-star service and—most important for some of their L.A. clients—privacy.

Celeste closed her eyes and sighed happily, thinking of the long summer days stretching in front of her. Lying out on her towel at the beach with Travis, hiking in the desert at twilight with Travis, watching trashy movies with Travis at his house in the afternoon. Then she sat up and shook her head. What the hell alternate universe was she in? She was going to be performing her usual six-days-a-week slog at the resort, folding towels and fetching water bottles, just like every summer. And Travis was going be two hours away, teaching surf lessons at the beach.

"Oh, Devon!" she wailed suddenly. A tiny white-haired

lady next to them shot Celeste an alarmed glance, then turned back to the digital camera she was holding and peered at it closely. Celeste watched the woman carefully press a button and take a picture, apparently of her lap. "I'm so sick of working every summer of my life," Celeste moaned. "I mean, I would've loved to go to that creative writing program I told you about, but—"

"What?" Devon's forehead wrinkled in concern. "I thought you hadn't said anything because you didn't get in."

"I didn't even apply." Celeste dropped her head on her friend's shoulder. "It wasn't worth it—Mom and Dad would never let me go. 'You have to save money for college,'" she mimicked. "Besides, I'd feel guilty for abandoning them during high season anyway."

Devon shook her head. "You're incredible. I'm lucky if I remember to say hi to my mom when I see her for the five minutes a day we're both in the house."

Celeste went on. "And I only have eighty-nine days until Travis leaves for Arizona State, and I'm not going to see him all summer! Then he'll go off to college and leave me behind, and meet tons of gorgeous sorority girls and never come to visit and forget all about me." She folded up her program and fanned her face. Not that it would do any good. The heat would have been unbearable even without the aid of whoever had doused themselves in Coco Mademoiselle perfume.

"Well, don't feel too sorry for yourself, drama queen. *I'm* going to be here too." Devon had a job as Pinyon's guest relations rep. She'd been wait-listed at a super-exclusive acting program in Scotland, so Celeste had convinced her to spend the summer making as much money as possible.

*Thank God*, Celeste thought a little guiltily. She knew how much Devon wanted to go to Glasgow, but at least she'd have someone around this summer other than her crazy parents.

The girls stopped talking as a tall man with a long red neck and a prominent Adam's apple appeared from behind the screen and made his way to the podium. He began harrumphing into the microphone.

"Hello? Hello? Is this on?" The microphone responded to his voice with an angry feedback whine. The audience covered their ears.

Mr. Ransick was the school board president. Every year, he and his wife spent their anniversary at the resort. They always ordered up champagne and strawberries, and Celeste, unfortunately, was usually the one to deliver them, which conjured up all sorts of images she'd rather forget.

A guy at a soundboard in the back fiddled with some dials and then nodded at Mr. Ransick.

"Okay!" Mr. Ransick said. "First of all, welcome to the sixtieth commencement exercises for the graduating class of Longbrook High School!" He paused to let a little ripple of applause scatter throughout the audience. Celeste opened her knockoff burgundy Marc Jacobs bag and checked her iPhone to see if Travis had texted. Nothing. She shifted on the hard plastic seat and surreptitiously tried to peel her dress off the back of her legs. Devon was tapping away on her BlackBerry.

"Who are you writing?" Celeste hissed.

"Stefan!" her friend whispered back. "I'm asking if he'll be at Kevin's after-party." A woman with a helmet of blond hair turned around and glared at them. Celeste shot her a gold-plated smile straight from Pinyon customer service.

Up front, Mr. Ransick was blathering on about commitment to their school's core values of equality, liberty, and paternity or something, and people were starting to shift around in their seats. Beside them, the white-haired lady took another picture of her lap.

"And without further ado . . ." Mr. Ransick seemed to be winding down. Celeste looked up. "Please welcome this year's graduating class." He gestured at the frizzy-haired school orchestra director at the front of the patio. The director raised her arms and the band struck up that perennial graduation favorite, "Pomp and Circumstance."

Celeste sat up in her seat, trying to spot Travis in the wobbly line of black-gowned seniors now gathered at the foot of the stage steps. Devon gasped.

"Look!" She pointed a pale pink–manicured finger at the stage.

A golf cart crammed with five guys wearing rubber monster heads and striped terry-cloth bathrobes accelerated up the wheelchair ramp onto the stage. A loud murmur rustled through the audience and a few people laughed. The music trailed to an uncertain halt as the orchestra director's waving arms wilted.

Celeste squinted her eyes. "What the hell?"

Devon was laughing next to her. "It's gotta be the senior prank! I can't believe they waited until the last possible day!"

The golf cart jerked to a halt in the middle of the stage. The five guys jumped out and lined up. In unison, they tore off their bathrobes and exposed matching purple, rhinestone-encrusted thongs. Mr. Ransick and the principal, Dr. Weaver, stood as if turned to stone. The microphone dropped from Mr. Ransick's slack hand and thumped to the floor with a loud whine. There was a moment of dead silence, and then all the students in the audience erupted with cheers. People started climbing onto their chairs and whistling. Some of the parents tried not to laugh, with varying degrees of success. The little old lady beside Celeste was sitting up very straight and frantically pressing every button on her camera as she finally aimed it toward the stage.

Celeste climbed up on her chair too, trying not to

break her ankle in her wobbly espadrilles. "Woo-hoo!" she yelled and took a couple of shots with her iPhone.

Suddenly, Celeste shrieked. She recognized two things a little two well: the swirling Pinyon Ranch logo across the side of the shiny white golf cart and the perfectly muscled chest of the tallest guy on stage, the one right in the middle.

Celeste shook Devon. "It's Travis!" she hissed, pointing frantically at the stage. "And that's *our* golf cart!"

"Oh my God," Devon said, gasping for air.

Mr. Ransick suddenly snapped out of his trance and ran toward the steps leading up to the stage. "Stop!" he shouted. He slipped on the pages of his speech, which had scattered across the stone patio, and fell heavily on his rear. "Call the police!" he yelled over his shoulder to no one. By now, everyone in the audience was on their feet. People were crowding the aisles trying to get a glimpse of the stage. Celeste clenched her teeth as she saw Dr. Weaver fiddling with a cell phone.

Up on stage, the guys draped their arms around each other's shoulders and began a Rockette-style kick line. They did a few do-si-dos, and then the audience screamed as Travis turned a cartwheel, nearly flashing two hundred parents and grandparents. In the distance, Celeste could hear the high blare of police sirens.

"Get out of there!" she moaned. "You're the world's biggest idiot! Go!"

The guys finished their dance and vaulted onto the golf cart, leaving the bathrobes heaped on the stage. Travis grabbed the wheel and floored the accelerator. The cart shot forward, but Travis lost control. With an awful cracking noise, he drove right off the side of the ramp. The audience, including Celeste and Devon, winced as the cart fell three feet down onto the patio, landing with a tremendous crash. The guys scrambled out and ran across the school lawn like crazed nudists, just as three police cars, sirens wailing and lights flashing, pulled up at the curb.

"Shit, Celeste!" Devon screeched, pointing at the crashed golf cart. Celeste followed her finger. There, next to the cart, struggling to his feet with his hand clapped over one eye, was Travis. Of course.

# Chapter Two

✦

Celeste gasped as the first cop reached her boyfriend. Yelling his name, she pushed through the thronging audience toward the front. The line of graduates at the side of the stage had deteriorated into a mob of black robes, all shoving one another to see what was going on. Behind her, the audience was roaring. As Celeste fought her way forward, she realized that she had no idea what she was going to do once she reached the stage. Grab Travis away from a police officer and spirit him away in the broken golf cart? *Celeste to the rescue!* Doubtful.

By the time she got to the front, Devon struggling behind her, a mustached young cop was already slapping handcuffs on her thong-clad boyfriend.

"Travis!" Celeste panted. He turned. The flesh around his right eye was already red and puffy, but his big dark eyes still managed to melt her. "You're hurt!"

"Hey, Celeste," he said weakly.

"Okay, let's go," the heartless policeman commanded. His mustache hung over his lip like a small, dead animal. "This one's got to come down to the station with me."

"Travis, are you being arrested?" Celeste squeaked. Travis and his friends had pulled stupid pranks all through high school, but no one had ever actually been *arrested* before. Usually the pranks just ended with parents coming home and yelling for a while.

"Uh . . ." Travis looked at the cop uncertainly.

"Well, we've got to hold him at the station until we can sort out what's going on here and track down his buddies," the cop said.

Travis looked over his shoulder as the cop hustled him toward the police cars at the curb. "Cel—will you come down to the station? I might need bail or something."

Celeste managed to nod as she watched Travis's bare butt cheeks make their way toward the cop car.

✦ ✦ ✦

Celeste gripped her bag nervously as she approached the beige cinder-block police station on Palmetto Drive. Her palms were slippery with sweat. Taking a deep breath, she swung open the heavy glass door. It closed behind her with a bang. The place seemed very quiet after the traffic noise of the busy street. An odor of gym shoes and bologna sandwiches hung in the air. Behind a scarred wooden reception desk, a middle-aged cop with gray hair looked up from his newspaper. "Help you?" he inquired, peering over his reading glasses.

"Um, yes, I'm here to see Travis Helding?" Celeste tried to steady her voice. She could feel goose bumps rising on her arms from the arctic air-conditioning.

The desk officer glanced at a thick sheaf of papers on a clipboard. "Room two. Just go down the hall, second door on the left."

"Thanks," Celeste said, summoning her Pinyon-employee smile for the second time that day. She started down a long, fluorescent-lit, linoleum-covered hallway. *Could this place* be *any more depressing?* she thought, stopping to moisten her dry mouth at the water fountain and noting the wad of old chewing gum stuck in the drain.

The first thing she saw when she pushed opened the door to room two was Travis, minus the handcuffs and now wearing what looked like orange hospital scrubs, sitting at a table in the middle of the room. He raised his head toward Celeste as she entered and grinned, his usual confidence apparently restored. His eye was now shiny blue-black and almost swollen closed. Even sitting in an interrogation room, he looked adorable. Celeste shot him a worried look and only then noticed the array of people seated against the walls of the room: Mr. Ransick, Dr. Weaver, and—Celeste gulped—her own mom and dad. The police must have called them. A suffocating silence lay over the room, broken only by the ticking of a wall clock. Celeste tried to arrange her face in a pleasant, serious, yet charming expression, but she knew she just looked vaguely stupid instead.

Meekly, Celeste crept over and took the seat next to her mom. She arranged her bag in her lap. Only then did she peek sideways at her parents. Her mom was shaking her head slowly back and forth with her lips pressed together, but her father . . . Celeste gulped inaudibly. Mr. Tippen's heavy dark eyebrows were drawn together, almost down to his nose, and his face was bright red.

Celeste stared straight ahead at the clock. Twelve fifty-five. After thirty seconds, she slid her eyes over toward her father. He caught her glance. "Hurrrrmm," he rumbled in his throat. It sounded like a diesel engine echoing against the cement walls.

Celeste looked at the floor. She'd helped Travis get out of trouble before, but that had been for stupid things like ditching study hall and letting the biology frogs out of their aquariums. Nothing that had involved actual law enforcement.

The wall clock ticked deafeningly. Twelve fifty-seven. The door flew open and everyone jumped. The mustached cop who had been at the school came in.

"Okay, everybody, I'm Officer Collins," he said, looking up from a clipboard of papers. Everyone sat up straighter, even Dr. Weaver. Travis folded his hands on the table in front of him.

Officer Collins seated himself at the table across from Travis, his heavy leather belt creaking with importance, and flipped through a few pages on his clipboard.

"Uh, let's see . . ." He squinted at some type and read in a monotone: "Travis Jason Helding, eighteen, charged with disorderly conduct, destruction of property and"— Officer Collins looked over at Mr. Tippen—"theft. I guess that was your golf cart, sir."

Celeste's father nodded grimly and tightened his arms over his chest. Travis's face was perfectly blank. He might as well have been listening to a lecture in class. *Remorse! Think remorse!* Celeste tried to mentally telegraph him.

Collins flipped to a blank form and poised a pen over it. "Okay, which of you is Dr. Weaver?"

"I am," Dr. Weaver said.

"All right, this young man is a student of yours?"

Dr. Weaver started to nod and then stopped. "Actually," he said after a pause, "he's not anymore. The diplomas are officially issued the day before the commencement exercises, which are merely a ceremony meant to—"

"Fine." The cop cut Weaver off. "So, you won't be expelling him?"

Mr. Ransick shrugged irritably. The skin on his neck looked redder than ever. "There's nothing we can do. It'll have to be up to the police." He looked hopefully at the cop.

Collins sighed. He turned to Celeste's father. "All right. Ah . . ." He glanced at his papers again. "Mr. and Mrs. Tippen. The golf cart was stolen from your property, the Pinyon Ranch. Would you like to press charges?" He looked at them expectantly.

Mr. Tippen opened his mouth to reply, but before he could say anything, Celeste leaped up from her seat, startling everyone in the room. "Dad!" she said, more loudly than she'd intended. All heads swiveled toward her. Collins rolled his eyes. "Can I talk to you outside for just a second?" She didn't wait for a response. "Great, thanks, we'll be right back, everyone." Everyone was staring at her. She flashed the room a toothy smile and grabbed her father by the arm, pulling him toward the door.

Outside in the hallway, Celeste faced her father. The fluorescent lights overhead glowed harshly, making him look old and tired. "What is it, Celeste?" he asked.

"Dad," she began, "I know Travis was an idiot.

Obviously." She carefully avoided the words *stole* and *criminal*. "But it was just a stupid senior prank. Please don't press charges! This is your own daughter's boyfriend!" Celeste clasped her hands together in front of her chest and tried to make her eyes as big as possible.

Her father sighed, rubbing his brown hair. "You know I've never particularly liked Travis. But I trust you, and I know you care about him. But now this . . ."

"Dad, come on—didn't you ever do anything stupid when you were young? Should you have gone to jail for it, really?"

Her dad's face softened for a moment. A small smile played across his face and she knew there was an opening. A teeny, tiny opening.

"See! Everyone does dumb things. Um—what if you think up some other punishment for Travis? Would that be okay?" Celeste resisted the urge to bounce up and down on her tiptoes.

Her father sighed. "All right, fine. You win. But"—he held up his finger as Celeste started to fling her arms around him—"he's still going to have to pay us back."

"Oh, I know." Celeste kissed her father on the cheek. "Thank you, thank you!"

Inside the room, everyone still looked like they were waiting for a funeral to start. Celeste tried to give Travis a thumbs-up sign with her eyes before hurrying back to her seat.

Her dad leaned over and whispered to her mother for a few seconds. "We've decided not to press charges for the theft of the golf cart," Mr. Tippen said aloud. Travis exhaled audibly and slumped back in his chair. "Instead, Travis will spend the summer working at the resort to pay off the damage. Three months of labor should take care of the cost."

Celeste couldn't stop her eyes from widening in excitement.

*What?* Travis at the resort? *All summer?* Celeste resisted the urge to leap onto the table and thank her dad all over again. Her father thought this was a *punishment?*

Travis made a strangled little noise and opened his mouth as if to protest. Celeste waved her hands at him frantically. *Shut up! Shut up!* she mouthed. He must have gotten the message, because he closed his mouth and aimed a feeble smile in the direction of her parents.

"Okay!" Collins stood up and tapped his papers into a neat rectangle. "Well, then, that's settled." He looked at Travis severely. "Mr. Helding, I never want to see you back here again."

"Yes, officer," Travis croaked as everyone stood up with a loud scraping of chairs. Dr. Weaver and Mr. Ransick nodded at Celeste's parents and quickly started down the hallway, leaving Celeste trailing behind with Travis.

He leaned close to her and she caught a whiff of his

Acqua di Parma aftershave. Even here, even with him wearing those ridiculous orange scrubs, knowing there was a purple thong underneath, she still wanted to throw herself at him.

"This sucks!" Travis whispered fiercely.

"I know," Celeste said automatically. Then she realized what he'd said. "Wait a minute—what do you mean, this sucks? You're going to be at the resort this summer. I won't have to drive up to the beach every weekend. We can be together!"

Up ahead, Celeste saw her father turn around. She dropped Travis's hand as if it were on fire and switched on her innocent, daughterly smile. Her father turned back forward and she grabbed Travis's hand again.

"Yeah," Travis muttered. "Working for free."

Celeste stopped walking. "Are you serious? You're not the tiniest bit happy you're going to see me all summer?" Her voice rose slightly and she saw her father hesitate. "I mean, that was a really rotten trick you pulled, Travis. How could you just destroy my family's property like that?" she said loudly. Her father started walking again.

Travis looked confused for a second and then draped his arm around her shoulder and pulled her into his side as they walked. "Look, I just have to get used to the idea, babe," he soothed her. "That's all." They had reached the glass doors to the outside. Celeste could see her parents getting into their old Volvo.

Celeste felt exhausted all of a sudden. She leaned her head against Travis's shoulder and looked up at his face.

"You're feeling bad about this summer, aren't you?" she said. She tried not to sound like she was accusing him of something.

"Nooo . . ." Travis said. He gazed at an auto body shop across the street. "I'm just figuring out how I'm going to tell Steve at the surf school that I'm basically under house arrest all summer."

"It's all right. Just tell him you got arrested for stealing a golf cart and doing a conga dance in a little purple thong. He'll totally understand," Celeste teased, lifting her head.

Travis snorted. "Thanks, babe. See, this is why I love you. You're so sweet."

He leaned in and pulled her toward him, his hand on the back of her neck. His stubble rasped against her face when he kissed her.

*She and Travis together at the resort all summer . . .* That prank might have been stupid, but it might also turn out to be just about the best thing to happen to their relationship.

# Chapter Three

✦

After spending graduation day party-hopping, Travis drove his purring BMW up to the darkened entrance of Pinyon to drop off Celeste and Devon. Two spotlights illuminated the low sandstone sign as Devon hopped out of the backseat.

"I'll give you kids a minute to say good night. See you up at the house, Celeste." Devon pranced up the drive barefoot, dangling her shoes in her hand.

The scent of the azalea bushes wafted into the car like thick perfume. Beyond the entrance, Celeste could see the bulk of the main building and the smaller shadows of the guesthouses as Devon skipped away from the car. Warm yellow lights glowed from the main building windows, which were open to catch the night air. A burst of jazz music floated down to them on the breeze. A trio always played in the lounge until two, for the guests who liked to relax with their drinks.

Celeste could just make out Travis's face. His dark eyes seemed huge. The lights from the dashboard illuminated his high, flat cheekbones. She leaned over the gearshift and pressed herself against him. A wave of warmth spread over her body as he pushed his hand under the hair at the back of her neck. She closed her eyes and felt his lips press against hers.

"I'm so glad you're working here this summer," she murmured.

"If the whole summer's going to be like this, I am too." His voice rasped in the darkness.

"Call me tomorrow?"

"Of course," he said, pulling her toward him for one last kiss.

Celeste waved to him from the entrance. The sleek metal gate slid shut behind her as she turned up the path toward the main building. She felt limp with exhaustion but content. For a day that had started off so completely terrible, it had turned out perfectly. Now she and Travis and Devon would be hanging out all summer long. Considering how not fun she'd expected the next three months to be, it kind of felt like she'd been handed an unexpected gift.

Celeste pressed the heels of her hands to her face as

she walked toward her parents' bungalow. Her cheeks were hot and she wondered if she was sunburned or still recovering from that nice little goodbye in Travis's car.

She pushed through the fence that surrounded the pool area. The surface of the water shimmered like a long sheet of turquoise silk, glowing with the yellow lights that lit it from underneath. All around the smooth teak patio, lounge chairs with white terry-cloth cushions stood ready, waiting for the next day's round of sunbathers and swimmers. At dawn, the pool attendants would place a fresh folded towel on each chair.

She followed the stone path around a clump of tall cypresses to the staff quarters, which included her parents' house. Celeste had lived in the little gray-painted bungalow since she was four years old, when her parents bought the resort. She had occasionally asked her dad why they couldn't move to a bigger place, but he always said that it was essential they live on the premises—he had to be available at all times in case there was a problem. Besides, he said, they worked for the resort just like everyone else. There was no need for them to live differently than the rest of the staff. Celeste still didn't see why she had to sleep in a room approximately the size of a shoe box until she went to college.

Her parents' bedroom window was dark, but they had left the porch light on. Celeste spotted Devon by the front door and held her finger to her lips. She eased the door open and the girls crossed the front hall, both careful to avoid the board in front of the coat closet that always creaked. The line under her parents' door remained black. With a sigh of relief, Celeste quietly shut the door to her room and fell on the bed. It wasn't like she had a curfew or anything, but if Dad woke up, he would come in and start going on about all the stuff she had to do tomorrow, and that was really the last thing she wanted to think about now. She just wanted to lie there and think about Travis's lips and his arms around her in the car. Celeste closed her eyes. Travis floated in front of her again.

Her musings were interrupted by Devon shivering.

"Can I borrow a sweatshirt?" In her silver minidress and slightly smudged smoky eye makeup, Devon resembled a cross between Victoria Beckham and Kurt Cobain. "You macked on your boyfriend for so long the wind made my buns feel like ice cubes."

"Hey, we could've dropped you off at home. You didn't *have* to sleep over." Celeste climbed out of bed. She stuffed her feet into a pair of furry moose bedroom slippers. Then she turned and gave her best friend a playful pat on the head. "But obviously I'm glad you did."

As soon as Celeste was up, Devon began burrowing under the comforter. "Mmm, it's so nice and warm in here." She closed her eyes and pulled the blanket up over her shoulder. Her face, with its mascara-ringed eyes and wild black hair, looked like that of a giant raccoon peering out from under the covers.

As Celeste stepped over Devon's discarded pink platforms, she noticed a piece of paper under them. She picked it up and groaned internally when she recognized her father's handwriting. The usual morning instructions. Dad must have pushed it under her door earlier in the evening. "Goodbye, carefree summer," she muttered to herself as she opened the sheet of scrap paper.

Celeste sat on the edge of the bed. "Move over," she said to Devon, who was already making little snoring noises.

"Mmmmm," her friend replied. She moved her leg a half-inch to the right.

Celeste lay back and scanned the note. *Celeste Tippen and Devon Wright: Instructions for Monday, June 20,* the heading said. Her dad had such a warm and fuzzy way about him. She read on. *Celeste: (1) Check and refill all towel stations with new Ralph Lauren towels. (2) Prep all cabanas: Evian spritzer bottles, water pitchers, Kiehl's sunscreen samples. (3) Prep for Saunders family arrival: check guesthouse, deliver fruit basket, greet car 10:30 a.m.*

Celeste bolted upright on the bed and let out a strangled squeak, like a mouse that had been stepped on. The note fluttered out of her limp hand onto the floor. "Devon!" she croaked in a strangled voice. "Devon, wake up! I'm in huge, giant trouble!"

"Mmmrrr?" Devon pushed open one eyelid. "What is it?" she muttered. "Have you been caught being criminally responsible again?"

Celeste shook her friend's shoulder. "Be serious! This is a major crisis!"

Devon rolled over onto her stomach. "Is it a major crisis that can wait until morning?" She pushed her face into the pillow.

"Nick Saunders!" Celeste stage-whispered. She kept an eye on the crack underneath her door. Still no lights came on.

"Who?" Devon peeked at Celeste with one eye.

"Nick Saunders! Remember, that guy who stays here every summer?"

"Kind of. Is he the one who's always bugging you to get him things?"

"Yeah, that's him. His family's from L.A.—his dad is some sort of big-time movie producer or something. Anyway, they're filthy rich and Nick totally knows it. He's always asking me to, like, get him this one special cheese sandwich from a place twenty-five miles away, and make sure it's on only white bread, extra mayonnaise—stuff like that."

"Riiiiight . . . I remember him now," Devon said. She propped herself up on her elbows. "Wait, hang on, didn't something happen with you and him last summer?"

Celeste closed her eyes and put a pillow over her face. "Yes."

"What? I can't hear you," Devon said. "Your voice is all muffly."

Celeste lowered the pillow slightly. "I said yes. We've always been superflirty with each other, and last summer we kinda hooked up. A few times. Okay, lots of times."

"You bad girl!"

"I wasn't bad! Travis and I had barely started dating. And it was *his* idea not to be exclusive while we spent the summer apart. I mean, I only saw him a few times while he was working at the surf school. And I know for a fact he dated other people."

"Well, what did Travis say about Nick?"

"Umm." Celeste paused. She was glad for the pillow on her face, because she could feel her cheeks flaming. "Actually, I didn't tell him. It was just a dumb flirtation followed by a convenient summer fling. But now they're destined to meet! If Nick is even one-third as obnoxious as usual, Travis is going to freak out. You know how jealous he can get."

"So does Nick, like, *like* you or something?" Devon asked.

Celeste snorted. She rolled onto her stomach and gazed out the window at her view of the storage shed. "Hah, no. He's just totally bored stuck out here in the desert. He needs a target for his flirting and I just happen to be here. I'm his distraction from hating summer. Or maybe I'm just practice for how he treats the girls in L.A. But I'm not sure I trust Travis to look past the 'I used to make out with your girlfriend' part of the situation."

Devon flopped back down and closed her eyes again. "Oh, don't worry about it. I'll be there to make sure everyone behaves themselves." She grinned.

"Yeah, sure—Devon Wright, moral guardian. Can't wait to see what your nun's cape looks like."

"Oh my God, that's brilliant," Devon mumbled. "That's my next Halloween costume—slutty nun."

"Good night, Dev."

Celeste heaved herself up from the bed. In her minuscule bathroom, she held her toothbrush under running water and gazed at her reflection in the mirror. Wide brown eyes and a worried frown stared back at her. Despite Devon's reassurance, if today was any indication of the emotional roller coaster she was going to ride this summer, there was a good chance not everyone would make it out alive.

# Chapter Four

✦

"Celeste! Wake up. It's nine forty-five! Where's Devon? They're asking for her in the office."

Celeste turned over and pulled the sheets over her head, hoping the ungodly banging and her mother's voice at the door would stop if she just ignored them both. But of course, that would have made this someone else's life. Next to her, Devon flopped around like a beached fish and groaned. Then, with a monumental effort, she sat up in bed.

"Hi, Mrs. Tippen!" she shouted through the closed door. "I'm here. I'll be down to the office in ten minutes, no worries!"

Mom's concerned voice continued. "The dining room's ending breakfast service in fifteen minutes. If you two don't make it, that's it until lunch."

Celeste bolted upright, swiping the hair out her eyes. "Okay!" she called. "We'll be right there."

Devon climbed out of bed and tried to smooth some of the wrinkles out of the silver minidress she was still wearing. Celeste eyed her friend. "Are you going to work in that?" she asked.

"No problem." Devon started rummaging in Celeste's closet. "I'm just going to borrow your black ballet flats and this wraparound top, okay?" She tied the black jersey top at the waist, slipped on the flats, and scraped her hair into a bun.

Celeste laughed. "You are amazing. How is it that you look like you've been planning that outfit for weeks?"

"Natural skill." Devon winked and opened the door.

"Hey, what about breakfast?" Celeste called after her.

"Can't." Devon's voice floated up the stairs. "It's my first day on the new job. . . ." Her words trailed off as the front door banged.

Celeste jumped out of bed and leaned out the open window to inhale the fresh morning air. The lemon sunlight spread over the white buildings of the resort and the desert beyond like icing. It was a gorgeous morning—the start of her first summer working with Travis! Well, working *near* Travis, Celeste amended to herself. Even if they were going to be in totally different jobs, he was here and that was what mattered. Celeste felt like doing a Julie Andrews "The Hills Are Alive" dance around the room, but breakfast was waiting. Travis's job didn't start until next week, so she pushed her lingering fear about a Travis-Nick showdown out of her mind for now. She took the world's fastest shower and plaited her hair into two long braids. Then she put on her white sleeveless polo shirt with the discreet Pinyon logo and her regulation khaki shorts. She didn't know why Mom had to choose Bermuda length for this year's uniform. It just made her legs look stumpy. Cursing Devon for having snagged the one non-uniform-requiring job at Pinyon, she stuck her feet into her Sperry Top-Siders and rubbed on a little M.A.C. Lipglass and some mascara.

In the spacious terra cotta–colored dining room, her father was sitting at his usual back table, papers and forms spread out everywhere. A cup of black coffee and a croissant with a single bite out of it were pushed to one side. Celeste collapsed in the chair across from him and picked up a piece of rubber tubing sitting on the table.

"What's this?" she asked.

"Sink piping," Dad answered, furiously signing a stack of invoices. "Harold ordered fifty of them and they're all the wrong size. Mrs. Klein called down this morning and said her sink was spraying all over the bathroom floor."

"Oh." Celeste was rapidly losing interest. She put the tubing down and looked around for breakfast. As if by magic, a skinny guy in a white jacket appeared next to her. "Oh, awesome, Rick! Thanks." Celeste could see the tattoos on the backs of both his hands as he set down a plate with a toasted bagel, cream cheese, and a dish of blueberries and punched Celeste lightly in the shoulder. "Solomon says to tell you that he only toasted your bagel because you promised to help him post that ad for his washing machine on Craigslist."

"Of course! We can do it this afternoon."

"Rick," Dad said, looking up with a frown, "all of the strawberries were wilted this morning. Remember we discussed the importance of garnishes at the last kitchen staff meeting."

"Yes, Mr. Tippen," Rick said seriously. Celeste caught his glance and rolled her eyes at her father.

"And please, for the last time, you need to remove your lip ring. Remember Pinyon dress code."

"Right, no problem." Rick hurried away.

Celeste took a huge bite of her bagel and followed it with a gulp of orange juice. Pinyon Ranch's trademark was fresh orange juice squeezed every morning from their own orange grove out back. It was one of Celeste's favorite things in the entire world.

"Celeste," her father said.

"Yeth?" she said through a mouthful of bagel.

"We need to go over the schedule for today." Her father pulled out a huge spreadsheet covered with tiny boxes showing everything that was happening at the resort that day and who was supposed to be doing what. "Now, the first thing—Larry and Kathy Saunders will be arriving in half an hour."

*Oh.* Celeste set down her bagel. Suddenly, it tasted like cardboard soaked in guilt.

"I need you to go over to the guesthouse this morning and check it. Everything should be ready, but I want you to place the welcome basket and our personal note to them."

"Okay," Celeste mumbled.

"Celeste."

She looked up. Dad set down his pen and slid his reading glasses onto the tip of his nose. Oh no. It was the "I'm going to tell you something very important that will require you to do a large amount of work" look. She'd been familiar with it since birth.

"The Saunders family are our best customers," Dad said. "Their happiness this summer is our number-one priority."

"Of course, Dad!" Celeste widened her eyes, hoping he wouldn't notice the blood draining from her face.

Her father knit his eyebrows. "Your mother and I are depending on you to help keep them happy and coming back. I want you to keep that in mind."

Celeste set down her spoon. She probably shouldn't eat any more blueberries considering the way her stomach was churning.

Dad went on. "Second thing. I've informed Jason that he should be on the lookout for Travis Helding at ten thirty sharp. They'll need to go over the procedure for—"

"Wait, what? I thought Travis wasn't starting until next week!" In fact, she'd been counting on having a few days to get things straight with Nick—as in, this summer, there was going to be *no* flirting and definitely no fooling around.

"He was, but Dominick dropped a mower engine on his foot this morning. He'll be out for the summer. I called Travis and told him he needed to start earlier than planned. You know that the grounds crew is the one area where we absolutely cannot be shorthanded." Dad looked up and caught Celeste's stricken stare. "I hope there aren't going to be any problems with Travis working here this summer. You know that I consider him an employee like everyone else—and subject to the same rules."

"Dad! You haven't even given him a chance yet," Celeste exclaimed. "You can't hold the golf cart thing against him all summer. Believe me, Travis is going to be awesome, I swear."

Her father raised his eyebrows slightly. "I'll believe it when I see it."

Celeste resisted the urge to roll her eyes and leaped up from the table, cramming the last bite of bagel into her mouth. Grabbing the welcome basket from the walk-in refrigerator in the kitchen, she hurried down the path to the guesthouses, oblivious to the deep blue desert sky arcing above and the palm trees waving gently in the salty, dry breeze. Around her, grounds crew workers were clipping the short, thick emerald grass or trimming juniper bushes into round spheres. Robe-clad women padded by in terry-cloth slippers, on their way to the spa for facials and massages. As Celeste rounded the pool, she could see the first batch of well-browned sun worshippers baking in the ninety-degree desert heat, the cool blue pool water spread beside them like an oasis. As usual, there was that one woman sitting under a pool umbrella, covered from head to toe in a long-sleeved cotton shirt, long cotton pants, huge sunglasses and, a sun hat. *Why does she even bother?* Celeste thought in spite of her rush.

At ten thirty sharp, she found herself standing next to her parents in the lobby of the main building, waiting to welcome the Saunderses. She fidgeted as the black Mercedes drew up in front of the bank of glass doors and a driver in a dark shirt jumped out. He opened the back door and Mr. and Mrs. Saunders appeared, both crisply dressed in white linen and hidden behind huge dark sunglasses. Then a shaggy blond head emerged, followed by perfectly toned shoulders in a Dries Van Noten shirt. Nick climbed out of the car and stood by the door, his bronze skin glowing in the sunlight. He might have been posing for a Ralph Lauren photo shoot. As Celeste watched, he drew a pair of Ray-Bans from the pocket of his khaki shorts and slid them on.

Celeste's face was flaming and her palms were sweaty. How could she have forgotten how hot he was? Her heart was thumping so hard beneath her polo shirt that she placed her hand on her chest to muffle the noise. *Okay, you've got to stop*, she told herself. *This is not right. No slobbering over Mr. Rich and Arrogant!* She took a deep breath and tried to shake off the creeping feeling that the summer had just gotten a lot more complicated.

The driver started lifting out suitcase after Louis Vuitton suitcase and lining them up at the curb as Mr. and Mrs. Saunders bustled inside. "Larry!" Mr. Saunders greeted Mr. Tippen, his tan, beefy hand outstretched. "Good to see you!" The two shook hands while Celeste's mom kissed pale, delicate Mrs. Saunders on her discreetly Botoxed and bronzered cheek. Celeste smiled and hugged Mr. Saunders. Mrs. Saunders gave her a kiss.

"Celeste, dear! You look lovely. Doesn't she, Larry?" she said, turning to her husband. "Lovelier every year."

"Mmm, yes," Mr. Saunders replied, nodding his dark blond head. Even with the slight puffiness of a middle-aged workaholic, his resemblance to his teenage son, with his chiseled jaw, was striking. "You're really growing up, Celeste. Turning into quite the lady."

Celeste wished everyone would stop talking about

how she looked, especially since Nick had come up behind his parents and was standing there with a typically flirtatious grin on his face.

"*I* think she looks lovely too, Mom," he said loudly, stepping forward. "Don't I get a hug?"

He put his arms around her and squeezed her tight. "Did I say 'lovely,' because I meant hot," Nick breathed suggestively into her ear. Before she knew what was happening, he'd lifted her high off the ground and planted a kiss on her forehead.

"Hey!" Celeste said, laughing and struggling to escape his grasp. "No harassing the employees!" As soon as the words were out of her mouth, her eyes locked on the doorway to the back patio. Travis stood just beyond Nick's shoulder wearing a green Pinyon staff shirt and a supremely pissed-off glare.

# Chapter Five

✦

Celeste's mouth went dry and she felt all her muscles clench, turning her into a stick of wood in Nick's arms. Sensing the change, he set her down and turned around, then smirked.

"Boyfriend?" he asked silkily. Travis had disappeared.

Celeste avoided his eyes. Her hands felt awkward all of a sudden, so she smoothed her hair to give them something to do. "I hope you're going to like the guest-house this year," she said to Mrs. Saunders. Even to her own ears, her voice sounded too loud and cheerful. Out of the corner of her eye, she could see Nick still watching her, a little smile curling the edges of his full-lipped mouth. She studiously ignored him. "We redid all the kitchens and bathrooms."

Mrs. Saunders was rummaging in her giant Marc Jacobs bag. "I'm sure it will be perfect, as always. Your parents do such a beautiful job here."

"Celeste."

She looked around at her father's voice.

"Would you mind just showing the Saunderses to their guesthouse and seeing if there's anything we can get them as they settle in?" her dad asked.

"Sure, Dad," Celeste said, betraying none of the urgency telling her to run away and find Travis as fast as she could.

She managed to avoid walking with Nick down the path to the guesthouse, since Mr. Saunders took her by the arm and made her tell him about school the whole way. Still, she could feel his eyes boring into her back at every step. When she turned around just once, he dropped her a wink as if to say he totally knew she was avoiding him.

"Ah, just as I remember it," Mrs. Saunders exclaimed as Celeste opened the front door. She inhaled deeply and stepped over the threshold into the cool, dim interior. Mr. Saunders brushed past, pulling his beeping BlackBerry out of his pocket. He went out onto the deck. "Get those contracts in the mail!" Celeste heard him say before he reached back and slid the heavy glass doors shut. She turned to go, but before she could, Nick caught at her arm.

She turned around. He just smiled and put his hands

in his khaki pockets. There was a long moment of silence. His eyes were so bright blue, they looked like chips of glacier. Celeste tried to hold his gaze, but it was too intense. She dropped her eyes.

"What?" she finally asked.

He smirked, infuriatingly still holding her arm. "I was just thinking about that night on the golf course—"

"Not happening, Nick. There will be no reliving of old times." She was impatient to leave. Travis was out there somewhere, getting more pissed off by the second.

"Oh, good. I prefer to try new things anyway. I had a thought. . . ." Was he deliberately taking his sweet time to get the sentence out or was it just her?

"Nick, I have a boyfriend. And I'd like to keep it that way. So this," she snapped, yanking her arm away from him and gesturing between the two of them. "This is going to be entirely professional this summer. You're a guest at my family's resort. That's all."

He widened his big sparkly eyes in mock dismay. "All I'm asking is if you could possibly bring me a sandwich from the kitchen—a fancy one with some sort of exotic-sounding cheese. And some fruit. And a Pellegrino with lime, if you have it. The drive up was really long, you know, and—"

Now Celeste could barely contain her annoyance. Which was actually kind of good, since the more irritating he acted, the easier it was to forget that he looked like a sun-bleached Zac Efron. "As you're fully aware, you can just call room service. It's *their* job," she added pointedly.

"Oh." He pouted for a second and then brightened. "Well, I'll call room service and ask if they can send you back with a sandwich for me. It's that personal attention, you know, that keeps us coming back year after year."

This time, Celeste just turned and walked out the door. She could hear him laugh behind her.

Celeste hurried down the path toward the maintenance sheds, panting a little in the hot sun. Her hair straggled out of its braids and clung sweatily to her forehead. She brushed through an opening in a tall hedge and came upon a small, plain wooden building. She peered through the open screen door where a tall man with a shock of wild gray curls was kneeling in front of an open file cabinet.

"Dave, have you seen Travis?" Celeste asked. The man looked up and a wide grin split his face. A gold front tooth glinted in the sun.

"Why are you so eager to find him?" he asked. He straightened up and grabbed a Big Gulp from the desk, noisily sucking up some Mountain Dew.

Celeste made a face. "That stuff is so nasty, Dave."

Dave grinned again. "Sixty-four ounces just isn't enough."

"So, um, have you seen Travis?"

Dave turned back to the files. "I sent that boy out with the mowing crew to break him in a little. They're doing the golf course."

Celeste groaned. The golf course was acres of rolling green hills, palm groves, and ponds. It would take her hours to find Travis out there. "Thanks, Dave," she called through the screen.

She trotted over the flat, grassy lawns, past the first sand trap and the caddy shed until, with relief, she saw the big green riding mowers circling the first hole. Travis's curly head bobbed on the seat of one. He seemed to be struggling with one of the gears. He shoved it and the mower stalled and then died. Travis gave the steering wheel a whack with his fist.

"Trav!" Celeste called out and waved. He looked up and then climbed down off the mower and kicked at one of the wheels before coming over.

Celeste quailed a little as he approached. She could tell by the vein throbbing in his forehead that he was still mad. Slowly, he walked over and stood in front of her, not saying anything.

She reached out and put her hand on his forearm. "Travis—look, I know you're mad about earlier."

He raised his eyebrows at her and looked away. Celeste rushed on.

"But it's not how it looks at all! That guy—that was Nick Saunders. He and parents have been coming here forever. They're our best customers. We've basically grown up together."

Travis was still gazing over the golf course. "Well, that didn't seem like a particularly brotherly hug." His voice was cold.

"Travis—look at me! He just grabbed me—I didn't even have time to react." She struggled to keep the tears out of her voice but her throat was swelling dangerously. "Look, don't be like this. I'm *not* interested in Nick Saunders. All I've been thinking about since yesterday is spending the summer with *you*. It's my job to be nice to him." She paused for a moment and took a breath. He bent down and peered into her face.

"Are you crying?" he asked, his forehead wrinkling.

"No," Celeste said, as a tear trickled down the side of her nose.

Travis wrapped his big arms around her and pulled her into his chest. Celeste buried her nose in his shoulder and inhaled his smell of cut grass, clean sweat, and Lever 2000 soap.

"Look, I'm sorry," Travis murmured into the hair at the top of her head. "I'm being a jealous jerk. I just hate thinking of you with anyone else. Can we forget I ever said anything?"

Celeste nodded. "That sounds great."

Travis slid his arm around her waist and started guiding her back to the grounds crew shed.

"Don't you have to keep mowing?" she asked.

Travis shook his head. "The gearshift's busted on that mower. I have to go tell Dave anyway."

They strolled together over the flat green desert grass. Celeste rested her head on Travis's arm. He took her hand and laced his fingers through hers. "Hey, let's take a lunch break and go get some food," he said.

Celeste hesitated. "Well, I'm not really supposed to take lunch until one. . . ." She stopped when she saw the laugh lines around Travis's mouth.

"Oh, you're having lunch with me," he said, his face splitting into a grin. "Right now. I'm kidnapping you for turkey sandwiches." In one movement, he scooped Celeste up in a fireman's carry and started trotting down the path. She shrieked, laughing hysterically, and beat on his back with her fists.

"Okay, okay, I surrender! I'll let you feed me," she yelled. She felt her foot hit something soft at the side of the path.

"Ooof!" someone said. Travis twirled around with Celeste still over his shoulder.

"Hey, sorry," Celeste heard him saying.

"Travis!" she whispered. "Put me down!"

He set her on her feet. Dave was standing in the middle of the path. Celeste hastily tried to tuck some of the hair back into her braids.

"Travis, I was just coming to find all of you guys,"

Dave said, wiping his hands on a rag. "Mr. Tippen's called an all-staff meeting for tonight. He wants to see everyone in the staff lounge after hours, nine o'clock. And, Celeste, there's a room service request that asked for you specifically."

Celeste felt the smile drop slowly off her face. She sighed and nodded. "Okay, Dave. I'll get right on it." So much for the brief escape. Back to Pinyon life.

# Chapter Six

✦

"C eleste!"

Celeste heard her name over the murmur of the packed staff room and whipped her head around. Through the rows of Pinyon employees, she could see Nick's arm waving from the first row. Celeste halted. Was he insane? Travis was standing right next to her! What was he doing at a staff meeting anyway? She glanced up at Travis. His eyebrows were raised but he wasn't saying anything . . . at least, not yet.

"Uh, here, Travis, you want to sit here?" Celeste pointed randomly at two chairs. If they sat down, they wouldn't be able to see Nick smirking at them.

"Everyone, everyone! Your attention, please." Dad was standing at the front. Celeste felt her phone buzz in her pocket and slid it out. Devon was texting her. Celeste kept one eye on her father and pressed read. CAN'T MAKE STAFF MTG—HANGING OUT W/ STEFAN. TAKE NOTES 4 ME!

Celeste stuffed her phone into her pocket. Great. Now she didn't even have Devon for moral support. At the front of the room, Dad had started talking.

"I've called this all-staff meeting to discuss an important and exciting event that is going to take place at the resort this summer, and which will require the help and cooperation of everyone here."

Celeste wondered what the heck her father could be talking about. Maybe they were finally going to install that infinity pool he'd always wanted. Except why would they do that in the middle of the high season? Maybe someone famous was coming to stay, like George Clooney or something.

"Many of you may know Larry Saunders and his wife, Kathy. They are not only longtime guests and dear friends of Pinyon, they are also movie producers with Blue Swan Productions in Los Angeles. Larry believes that Pinyon has a lot to offer his most recent venture—a new film festival held"—he paused dramatically—"right here at Pinyon Ranch!"

Everyone gasped, and whispers and murmurs ran through staff. Then Rick started applauding, followed by the rest of the staff. Mr. Saunders took the floor, giving details about when the festival would be, how many days it would last, and what kinds of parties were planned for the different films, but Celeste barely heard him. Holding a festival would mean that every guesthouse would be packed, and not just with average rich folks from L.A. Instead, they'd get all the Hollywood types: producers, directors, stars, and all of *their* guests. This was the kind of event that could move Pinyon from a minor player on the A-list to the very top. Basically, this festival was going to be the best thing to happen to the resort in its entire existence. And, she realized, a ton of work.

Celeste's dad stood up at the front again. "Thank you, everyone, for your patience. Enjoy your evening."

There was a general scraping of chairs and chattering as everyone got up and started collecting their things. Celeste turned to her boyfriend, but before she could say anything she noticed with dismay that Nick was making his way through the crowd over to them.

"Uh, Travis!" she said suddenly. "Hey, look, Rick's waving at us. Let's go see what he's up to tonight." She grabbed Travis's muscular forearm and tried to pull him toward the door.

"Isn't this awesome news, Celeste?" Solomon, the cook, bobbed up in front of them, a grin stretching his broad face.

Celeste tried to do a feint around him. "Yeah! Yes! It's totally cool, Solomon. Very exciting." She could see Nick's blond head getting closer.

"Hold on, Cel. I dropped my keys," Travis said. He bent over to retrieve them as Nick bounded up. Trapped, Celeste stood helpless.

"Hey, beautiful," Nick said. He was wearing a slim gray T-shirt that clung to his wiry shoulders, and his blond hair was falling into his eyes as usual. Travis froze, his back to them. Slowly, he turned around. Celeste winced. She could already see the warning vein starting to throb in the middle of his forehead. Celeste stepped in front of him. "Hi," she said in what she hope was a friendly but politely distant voice. "This is my, uh, boyfriend. Travis."

Nick didn't even glance at Travis. Instead, he fixed his eyes on Celeste's face. "I'm really glad you're going to be here to help with the festival, Celeste," he said, dropping his voice a little and putting his hand on her shoulder. She could feel his breath on her cheek and stepped backwards suddenly, almost stumbling over one of the folding chairs. Unbelievable—was he actually·flirting with her *right here*?

She heard Travis make a rumbling noise next to her, kind of like a bull clearing this throat. She darted a quick glance at his face. The vein was going into throbbing overdrive now and his dark eyes looked almost black. Not a good sign. *Defuse, Celeste! Defuse!*

She reached down deep and pulled up the most plastic Pinyon customer service smile she could muster, the one born of ten solid years dealing with difficult guests.

"Yeah, the festival's going to be great," she said smoothly. No one would ever have guessed her hands were shaking worse than a heroin addict's. "We're lucky to have your parents sponsoring it. They're amazing."

Travis let out another bull rumble. Celeste switched into high gear.

"Okay! Well, we're heading out, so see you later, Nick." She turned and grabbed Travis with the intention of shoving him toward the door with all the strength in her body.

"I'm mostly glad because I want you to help me plan my screening party for the festival," Nick said smoothly. Celeste stopped and turned around again slowly.

There was a moment of dead silence. "Ah, what do you mean, *your* party?" Celeste asked carefully.

"You know, for my film." Nick stuffed his hands in his pockets and blinked innocently.

Travis spoke for the first time. "What are you talking about?" His gruff voice was decidedly confrontational. Celeste winced. But Nick acted like Travis had just asked him to hang out sometime.

"I took this elective film studies course at UCLA last winter and the final project was making our own short films—writing, directing, editing, everything. My dad told me I could throw a screening party during the festival. But I've got to do all the organizing and planning myself, and you know, I'm not very good at that stuff.

That's why I'm really looking forward to us working together, Celeste." He fixed his gaze on her again as if she were the only person in the room and gave her a small smile. The rumbling bull that was her boyfriend took a step forward. Oh crap.

Celeste narrowed her eyes. "Whatever, Nick. Obviously, someone in guest relations will assist you with your planning." She tried to make her voice as frosty as possible.

"Good," Nick replied, apparently unfazed. "I'll definitely need help—*your* help." He offered them a relaxed grin. "Excuse me." Celeste stepped aside as he brushed past, but he still managed to rub right up against her, his arm trailing against the small of her back. Suddenly, Travis let out a growl and lunged for Nick.

"Travis!" Celeste dove for his arm and hung on to it with all her body weight. Nick was casually ambling away down the aisle like nothing had happened. She clung to Travis's arm and gazed up at his face. He was breathing like a diesel truck and his whole face was bright red, except for the edges of his nostrils, which were white. He looked down at her and took a deep breath. She leaned up against him. "You want to come for a walk? I need some air."

He nodded, and together they made their way through the emptying room and pushed out the door into the cool desert night. The quiet grounds were full of dark shadows, and their feet left silvery footprints in the cool, dewy grass. A half-moon floated in the black sky overhead.

Travis took Celeste's hand and swung it back and forth as they walked. His good humor seemed to have been restored now that he was removed from Nick's presence.

"Must be nice to get your own screening party just because your rich dad is throwing a film festival, huh?" he said.

"Yeah," Celeste agreed. To herself, she thought about what might be possible if she had some big-time New York editor father. Forget writing workshops in the Berkshires. She'd be straight on to an internship at *Harper's*. Goodbye family business, goodbye towel-folding, hello real job.

"You know," she said slowly. "I wouldn't even know what to do with myself, working someplace other than here. I've never even had a real job." She'd never actually said that out loud before.

"Hmmm?" Travis was watching a couple splashing in the pool as they passed. "What did you say?"

"Nothing."

Travis looked down at her. "No, really, what did you say?"

She took a deep breath. "I said that I've lived in this Pinyon bubble, like, my whole life. What's going to happen to me when I finally escape?"

Travis looked confused. He shook his head. "I don't get it. What do you mean, what's going to happen? You'll just leave, like everyone else."

Celeste shook her head. "No, you don't get it—"

Travis interrupted her by sliding an arm around her waist and pulling her close. He bent his head down to hers, but she drew away.

"What?" he said.

"Someone could come by," she whispered, gesturing around them. As if on cue, a man in a suit with the tie pulled down came around the corner and glanced at them curiously before disappearing into the lounge. A burst of voices and music floated out to them as he opened the door.

Travis looked impatient. "Well, then let's go hang out on the golf course. No one's going to be out there at ten o'clock."

"Okay," Celeste started to agree, and then an idea hit her. "Hey, you want to see my secret spot?"

Travis shrugged. "Sure."

Together, they tramped over the manicured grass of the golf course, past a pond and a sand trap until they reached the other side, where the desert plants still grew wild and tangled. She glanced around once and, seeing no one, bent down and pushed through a huge stand of prickly bushes. "Hey!" Travis whispered. "I can't get in there."

"No, you can," Celeste answered. "It's not as thick as

it looks." She held the branches apart and peered through the opening at Travis. "Come on!"

He looked doubtful but bent down and climbed through, trying not to get snagged on the twigs. Once inside, he looked around. "This is cool!" he exclaimed.

"Yeah, I know," Celeste said. Though it only looked like a scrubby tangle from the outside, the bushes actually surrounded a perfect circle of closely spaced palmetto trees, making a thick screen so that no one could see in from the outside. In the middle of the scaly trunks was warm, smooth sand lying in ripples. Celeste sank down onto her knees. The air was warm and still and the sand felt like silk against her bare legs. She looked up at Travis, still standing above her. "Come here," she said, reaching up and tugging at his hand.

Awkwardly, he thumped to his knees next to her.

Suddenly, an idea flashed through Celeste's mind. "Look, don't worry about Nick," she said, squeezing Travis's hand. "Devon is the guest relations rep. That means *she* should have to deal with the whole party situation, not me. I'll just tell her that's one of her new assignments. She'll love it. And Nick can have a great new target for his obnoxiousness too. I wouldn't be surprised if we barely see him again all summer."

Travis shrugged. "I don't care what happens, as long as he stays away from you," he said. Then he leaned over and wrapped his arms around her. She shivered at the friction of his skin against hers. He kissed her slowly and she felt a little jolt of electricity run all through her. The stubble on his chin rasped against her skin. The stress of the meeting began to float away. It was just her and Travis now, floating together on a bed of soft, warm kisses that were making her body go all limp and—

Travis drew his head away.

"What?" Celeste asked, her eyes still closed. "Is someone coming?"

"Are you sure there's never been anything between you guys?" Travis asked. Celeste opened her eyes. "Because he sure acts like he's more than just a customer."

*Poof.* The bed of warm kisses disappeared. Celeste shifted her knees. There was a palmetto frond poking her in the back. "Look, don't worry about it," she soothed, reaching for Travis again. "I'm sure once he meets Devon, everyone will get along a lot better."

For a long moment, Travis didn't reply. "Okay," he finally said. "But that doesn't mean I have to like him." He lay back on the sand, pulling Celeste down with him.

As she lay in her boyfriend's arms, staring at the black velvet night sky above them, Celeste thought that she might as well forget about towel-folding for this summer. Obviously, she had a much more important job in front of her: stopping Travis from bashing Nick's face in.

And stopping Nick from acting like she was standing in front of him naked. Oh yeah, and keeping the Saunders family happy, at peril to her life. Maybe she should've taken a job as secretary of defense this summer. It would probably be easier than this.

# Chapter Seven

✦

"Okay, I'm ready!" Celeste called, hanging upside down by her knees from a low tree branch. Her braids almost brushed the ground. "Hurry up, Travis, all the blood is rushing to my head." She could feel the scaly branch pressing into the backs of her knees as she gazed at the inverted golf course.

The mid-afternoon sun was bright and glassy. The contrast between the green of the golf course and the brilliant blue of the sky almost hurt to look at. A few lone golfers were trailing across the seventh hole, but Celeste and Travis were safely hidden in the scrub on the far side. No one would come over here unless he or she was a spectacularly bad golfer.

"Hold still," Travis said, aiming the camera. "All

right, got it." He pressed a few buttons and studied the shot. "Cute. You look hot with your face all red and squished up like that."

Instead of answering, Celeste swung back and forth a few times and then with a giant heave pulled herself up so she was lying on her stomach on top of the branch. "Thanks," she said, looking down at Travis's head below her. "You know, I have a direct hit on you from up here."

"Not for long." Suddenly, Travis tossed the camera straight up in the air. Celeste shrieked and stuck out her hand, just barely managing to catch it. Travis scaled the tree trunk and hoisted himself onto the branch next to her.

"Fancy meeting you here," he said, leaning over to nuzzle her neck. Celeste giggled and leaned back.

"Okay, smile," she said. Travis propped himself against the tree trunk and winked at the camera.

Just as she was about to press the shutter, her radio crackled. "Damn!" Celeste stuck the camera in her pocket. "I knew they'd find me."

"That's what you get for sneaking off when you're supposed to be working, you slacker." Travis grinned and yawned. He slid off the branch onto the sand and stretched his arms over his head. "I think it's almost time for my nap."

Celeste unclipped the radio from her belt and pressed speak. "Yes?"

"Celeste, this is Rick," a voice crackled through the speaker.

"Yeah?"

"A guest at the Saunders guesthouse would like you to bring over . . ." Celeste quickly glanced down at Travis to see if he had heard *that name*, but luckily his eyes were still closed. She turned down the volume on the radio and pressed it against her ear.

"Ah, here it is." Rick apparently found his list. "Two towels, one glass of Perrier with lemons but no ice, a slice of wheat toast with butter and strawberry jam, and a copy of *Us Weekly*." He paused. "Celeste?"

"Yes, I'm here," Celeste said into the radio, resisting the urge to bang her head against the tree branch. *Us Weekly?* What did he think she was, a flight attendant? "Look, Rick, just tell him—" Her father's voice suddenly boomed in her head, like some sort of edict from God: *Keeping the Saunders family happy should be your number one priority.* Celeste gritted her teeth and sighed. "Rick?"

"Still here."

"Tell the, ah, *guest* that I'll be right over." She slid down from her tree perch and landed with a thump next to Travis.

"Mmm," he muttered without opening his eyes. "Definitely nap time. Come here." He reached for her but she stood up.

"Trav, I have to go deal with a guest situation. Rick just called over on the radio."

"No, don't go," Travis said dreamily. "So nice here in the sun. Let's just chill for a minute."

Celeste smiled. His brown curls were falling over his forehead and his cheeks were flushed like a little boy's. "I can't, I have to go," she said softly.

To her surprise, Travis opened his eyes and heaved himself up. "Yeah, I should probably get back too. Dave's going to come check up on me any minute." He reached out and brushed some grass off Celeste's rear. "I'll walk you to your errand." He turned and started heading across the golf course.

Celeste's hands went cold. She bounded after him. "Ah, Travis, wait," she said, panting a little as she tried to keep up. "That's okay. You don't have to walk me. You should definitely get back. Dave'll find you slacking off otherwise!" She tried to sound as casual as possible.

Just then, her phone buzzed in her pocket. She whipped it out and shot a glance at the screen. Nick. She pressed mute and dropped it back in her pocket. They were almost back at the main building now. Celeste could see the swimmers in the pool, their bathing suits bright splashes of color against the turquoise water. *Buzz-buzz.* Her phone again. Travis glanced at her.

"Why don't you answer that?" he asked.

"Oh, um, it's probably a telemarketer or something," Celeste fumbled. Travis wrinkled his forehead.

"On a cell phone?"

*Buzz-buzz. Damn it, Nick!* She flipped open the phone.

"Hey, baby," Nick's voice said on the other end. *Baby?!*

Celeste glanced at Travis. "Oh, hello, Mr. Juarez," she said loudly.

"Who's Mr. Juarez?" Nick asked. "Are you bringing over the stuff I ordered?"

Celeste gritted her teeth. "Of course, sir," she said into the phone. "I'd be glad to recommend a few restaurants for your anniversary."

"Huh?" Nick said. "Are you whacked?"

"Certainly, sir," Celeste warbled. "I'll have them for you by the end of the day." She clicked her phone closed and mopped at the sweat trickling down her forehead. Travis stopped. They were next to the grounds shed.

"Okay, so see you later?" he asked, leaning down to kiss her.

"Definitely," Celeste replied. She darted a quick glance around for any parental-figure types and then planted a lingering kiss on his mouth. Dave appeared at the screen door of the shed.

"Trav!" He waved. "I need you to get on that weed-whacker, stat. All the edging on the main paths."

Travis nodded dutifully. He gave Celeste a squeeze and headed inside, letting the door bang shut behind him.

*Whew!* Celeste took a deep breath as she hurried to the pool for water and towels. That could have gotten very ugly. She threw a few towels and a glass of water onto a tray (forget the toast, she wasn't going to start making his breakfast) and hustled down the path to the Saunders villa, the Perrier slopping out of the glass with every step. She skirted the main building and headed through the palm grove. She was just rounding the bend when she spotted a tall, white-shirted figure puttering along the path, weed-whacker in hand.

Travis! His name flashed in Celeste's mind in big red letters. The figure ahead of her stopped to examine his machine and Celeste saw her chance. Still balancing the tray of towels and water, she jumped behind an azalea bush at the side of the path and crouched down. She peered through the skinny leaves in front of her. The dirt behind the bush smelled sour, and a mosquito buzzed up to investigate. Celeste swatted at her ear. A woman's heels clicked down the path and Celeste glimpsed a pair of gold sandals going by. Not Travis, obviously. Where was he? Communing with his weed-whacker?

Her right foot was going to sleep. Gingerly, Celeste tried to shift her cramped position. The mosquito bit her viciously on the lower back where her shirt had ridden up. She reached around to smack it but fell backwards onto the tray instead. "Shit!" Celeste whispered. The glass had tipped over, soaking the towels, which were now scattered with mulch. Not the most appealing setup, but then again, not the biggest of her worries right now.

Just then, to her immense relief, Celeste heard the weed-whacker start up out on the path. The noise grew closer and after a minute she could see Travis's size-fourteen New Balances coming slowly down the path as he guided the weed-whacker along the grass at the edge. The machine noise grew almost deafening, and Celeste wrinkled her face as Travis carefully guided the weed-whacker right along the grass by her azalea bush. She held her breath, despite the grass blades now spraying her face, and let it out only when he had moved on and the machine noise had faded to a safe distance. She rested her forehead on her knees. This kind of stress surely wasn't good for her complexion.

Celeste extracted herself and her disgusting tray from the bushes, trying not to fall over on her tingling right foot. She took a deep breath and balanced the tray on a pillar for a minute while she tried to smooth her now-wild braids with the palms of her hands. Whatever. Maybe Nick would lay off once he saw her looking like such a crazy lady.

As she walked up the path to the Saunderses' front

door, she noted that the black Mercedes was gone from the driveway. *Just deliver the empty water and the soaked towels and get out of here*, she told herself. *Thirty seconds. No more.* She knocked carefully. There was no answer, but the door was ajar, so she cautiously pushed it open. "Hello?" she called, just in case Nick's parents were there. "It's—"

"Back here!" Nick's voice came from the back deck. Celeste made her way through the cool, airy rooms to the back. The guesthouse the Saunderses were in was the only one that came with its own private pool made totally of desert sandstone. One of the Pinyon bathrobes was thrown over a beach chair pushed askew on the deck. Celeste could see Nick's figure bobbing in the turquoise water.

"Hey!" he greeted her enthusiastically. He swam to the side of the pool and rested his tanned arms on the edges.

"Hi," Celeste said warily, as she set the tray down on a side table. "Here's your stuff."

"Thanks," Nick said, not even glancing at the tray. He stared up at her. His straight blond hair was plastered to his forehead and he wore a pair of baggy navy swimming trunks. In one clean motion, he hoisted himself out of the pool, the wiry muscles in his arms flexing, and stood in front of Celeste, dripping and panting. She couldn't help notice that even though he was skinny, his abs and chest muscles were clearly defined and his shoulders were broad and strong looking. Celeste realized she was staring and looked away.

"Well, I'm really busy," she said, turning away, "so have a good swim and—"

"Wait!" Nick said. Celeste turned back.

"What?"

"Don't you want to go for a swim? My parents are gone all day and we could order lunch. . . ."

Celeste had to consciously restrain herself from rolling her eyes. "Nick," she said, as if talking to a kindergartener, "I'm *working* right now. That's like a job, you know? Actually, maybe you don't know." It came out a little harsher than she intended and a faint frown crossed his face. "And shockingly," she said, softening her tone, "I didn't think to bring a bathing suit."

Nick smiled devilishly. His perfect teeth flashed in the sun and his blue eyes crinkled at the corners. He stepped a little closer and Celeste caught a whiff of deodorant and warm skin. She felt her skin prickle at his nearness and inhaled sharply. "So what?" he said, grinning. "We don't need suits. . . ."

Celeste jerked her head back and suddenly realized how close they'd been standing. She stepped backwards, fast.

Nick laughed. "Or we could just play Scrabble," he said, collapsing gracefully onto a lounge chair. "Strip Scrabble."

Celeste gave him her dirtiest look and spun on her heel, marching through the empty guesthouse without looking back. She knew that if she did she'd see Nick staring after her with his nuclear-powered grin. "Nuclear" was also a good description for what Travis's reaction would have been to that little conversation.

Celeste stalked down the path, barely managing to fire a pleasant Pinyon-employee smile at an old lady tottering by with a walker. She blew air out of her nose like an elephant, trying to calm her pounding heart.

As her heart rate slowed, she felt her phone vibrate. Damn it! He just never quit! Forget Dad's warning. This was too much. Celeste grabbed the phone out of her pocket and flipped it open so hard she almost broke it off its hinges.

"No!" she shouted. "No, I am not bringing over more towels! Or swimming with you. Or skinny-dipping. Not now or ever!"

There was a moment's silence on the other end.

"Okay," a voice said dubiously. "But are you sure about the skinny-dipping?"

Celeste stopped walking. "Oh my God. Devon?"

"Yeah," Devon said. "Now will you go skinny-dipping with me?"

Celeste's knees felt weak and wobbly. "I've just had the worst half hour you can ever imagine," she said, now walking very slowly, like an old, old lady.

"Well, it's about to get a little worse. You have to get over here ASAP. Travis is out back asleep and your dad was just in the office, asking where he was. He's gone to look for him."

"Damn it! Distract him, do something!" The only thing worse than having Travis and Nick in the same place all summer would be not having Travis around at all. And while "sleeping on the job" wasn't specifically on her father's list of fireable offenses, Celeste was pretty sure it went without saying.

"I can't, he just left."

"I'll be right there." Celeste clicked her phone shut and broke into a run.

# Chapter Eight

✦

Celeste flew down the path to the main building, almost
knocking over two of the sous-chefs wheeling a tower-
ing pink-frosted cake toward one of the guesthouses.

"Hey, Celeste!" one of them called after her, but she
didn't turn around.

*What was he thinking?* she wondered as her deck shoes
pounded the red sandstone. Now Travis would be fired
and go back to the beach and she'd see him twice all
summer! Or Travis would be fired and her dad would
sue him for the golf cart money and he wouldn't be able
to pay it, so he'd have to go to jail instead of Arizona,
and she'd still never see him. Or . . .

Celeste skidded around the corner of the kitchen off
the main building. Travis lay peacefully under the big

tree, his arms stretched over his head and the cool green light from the leaves flickering over his face.

"Travis!" Celeste hissed as loud as she could. "Wake up!"

He opened his eyes slowly and smiled dreamily. "Celeste," he mumbled. "You're here. I was having a dream. . . . You were there. You were wearing this red silky thing . . . and cowboy boots." He propped himself on his elbows. From behind her, Celeste heard the kitchen door bang.

"Get up, get up, get up!" she whispered frantically, tugging at Travis's hand. "My dad!"

His eyes snapped open like window shades and he scrambled to his feet. "Your dad?" he said, whipping his head around. "Where?"

"Here, now!" Celeste thrust the discarded weed-whacker into his hand and pressed the start button just as she heard her father's voice from behind her.

"Travis, I was just looking for you."

Celeste turned around. Travis was industriously whacking the grass around her feet. He straightened up, wiping his forehead as if he'd spent the last half hour trimming every blade of grass at Pinyon.

"Hi, Dad," Celeste said, wondering how her voice could sound so calm when her heart was still throwing itself wildly against the inside of her rib cage, like some sort of crazed hamster.

"Hey, Mr. Tippen," Travis said, breathing heavily.

"Hello, Travis," Celeste's father answered, eyeing Travis's grass-stained work boots and tucked-in polo shirt. He gave a tiny nod of approval that only Celeste caught. She smiled to herself.

"I wanted to give you this." Mr. Tippen extended a piece of paper. "I had Jeannette draw up a record of how many hours you've logged so far toward your debt."

"Cool. Thanks, Mr. Tippen." Travis folded up the paper into a tiny square and stuck it in his pocket. Dad frowned faintly.

"Are you going back to the office, Dad?" Celeste asked. He glanced down at the stack of papers in his hand.

"Yes, I just came out to see how you were doing. I have a meeting with Solomon about the menu for the month—we're switching over some of the entrees. Fresh fish has gone up exorbitantly at the market."

"I'll walk with you," she offered. She waved to Travis and started heading down the path with her father.

As they strolled, Celeste cast a sideways glance at her father from under her eyelashes. "So, Travis hasn't worked off the golf cart yet?" she asked after a minute.

Her father snorted. "He's got a ways to go on that one. If I were making him pay us in money instead of labor, it would take a lot longer than three months for him to earn enough." Then his tone softened as he put his arm around his daughter. "I have to admit, though, he's been a good worker. Dave says he's really taken to mowing, even in this heat." Her father glanced at her. "Maybe I've been a little hard about him in the past."

Celeste laughed. "A *little*? Maybe if you're Genghis Khan. He really is a good guy, Daddy. I've been trying to tell you that all year."

Her father smiled and kissed her on the top of her head. "Well, we'll see. The summer's not over yet." He swung the glass door to the main building open and disappeared inside. Celeste watched him go, and when the door had swung safely shut, she doubled back to the big tree. Travis was attacking the tall grass by the kitchen door with his back to her. She crept up behind him and smacked his butt.

"Hey!" He whirled around.

"Don't turn the weed-whacker off," she said quickly. "Dad's still inside. But do you want to go for a swim tonight?" she asked. The engine noise and the odor from the kitchen Dumpster were making it hard to be seductive, but she was doing her best.

A grin split Travis's face. "Do you even need to ask?"

"Okay. Meet me at midnight at the pool gate. It'll be totally empty at that hour."

Just then Celeste's phone buzzed again. She glanced at it. Nick.

Playfully, Travis craned his head. "Who's calling, your boyfriend?" he teased. Thank God he couldn't see the screen.

"Oh yeah, right!" Celeste said quickly. She forced an idiotic little giggle. Travis gave her a strange look but leaned down and kissed her quickly.

"See you tonight."

✦ ✦ ✦

Celeste felt good when she showed up at the pool gate that night, wearing her new H&M bikini under a loose cotton beach dress. She deserved a little fun after her day of insanity. But she could see Travis was in a rotten mood the minute he walked up. He grunted in response to her greeting, without kissing her, and then when went straight to the pool and dove in. Celeste followed. The icy blue water felt fantastic against her dusty, hot skin.

She paddled over to the side, where Travis was resting his arms on the pool edge and gazing moodily out at the road, a sliver of which was just visible beyond the main gate. Celeste swam up behind him and softly ran her hand over the hard muscles in his back and shoulders. "What's wrong?" she asked.

He shook off her hand. "Nothing–I'm fine." Almost angrily, he stroked to the other side of the pool. Celeste swam back and forth a little and then paddled over to the steps. She climbed up on the first one and sat down, looping her arms over her knees.

Travis turned around. "Look, it's just that Kevin told me today that the surf instructors at the beach are all hosting Derek Rodham next week."

Celeste must have looked blank because he burst out, "He's like the biggest surfer on the West Coast! They get to surf with him and take a class. And I'm missing it because I'm stuck here in the desert!" He struck the water with his fist.

"That sucks. I'm sorry," Celeste said softly. To herself, she thought that Travis should just man up. It was his stupid prank that had gotten him here anyway. And besides, wasn't he glad that *she* was here? "Anyway," she said, pushing off the step and swimming over to him, "let's forget about that. Give me a ride!" She jumped on his back.

At first, he didn't move. Then he grabbed her arms, held them around his neck, and dove under the water. He swam the entire length of the pool and then, just when Celeste thought she was going to choke, he surfaced. Spluttering, she gasped a lungful of air. "That was so long!" she said, flipping around so she could face him.

He smiled grudgingly. She wrapped her arms around his neck and her legs around his waist, while he backed up against the pool wall. "Don't think about any of that stuff right now," she said softly, touching his cool lips with her mouth. He closed his eyes and nodded, running his hands up her wet arms. He slid them down her back and she pressed herself more tightly against him. His mouth pressed more firmly on hers and she shivered as the warm night breeze played over her shoulders.

"You're right," he said, drawing back after a long moment. "You're here, I'm here. I don't care about anything else." His breath tickled her cheek.

"That's right," Celeste whispered. "Nothing else matters."

# Chapter Nine

✦

Celeste sat at one of the desks in the main office a few days later, trying to figure out how many flower arrangements she needed to order for the wedding shower Mrs. Anderson was hosting for Taylor Hargrove, the daughter of one of the biggest restaurant entrepreneurs in L.A. Celeste stared down at the diagram of the Silver Room spread out in front of her and erased the little table sketch she'd just drawn. She took a swig of her caramel latte and glanced at her watch. Travis was supposed to come by once he was done mowing down by the main gates. Celeste erased another table and blew the dust off the desk, wondering idly how Travis could stand sitting on that smelly mower all day in the hot sun.

At least the office was quiet and cool. Her mom and dad were in town, meeting with their accountants. Even the secretaries were gone. The computer system had gone down this morning, so Dad had given everyone a few hours off until the guy from IBM came.

As Celeste bent close to the sketch and carefully drew in another table by the wall, the door clicked open behind her. She smiled to herself and pretended to concentrate. Footsteps crept across the carpet behind her and stopped. Celeste could sense someone standing right behind her chair. A pad of paper landed on the desk next to her. Celeste dropped her pencil and, without looking around, stretched her arms up and back, grabbing the person around the waist. "Hey, baby," she said.

"Wow, this is a nice change," a voice said. Celeste suddenly realized that the person she was grabbing was much skinnier than Travis, and the voice wasn't as gravelly. She jumped and her knee jarred the desk, spilling her cardboard cup of coffee—all over Mrs. Anderson's seating plan. "Damn it!" she yelled, and leaped up.

"Oops! Sorry," Nick said.

"What the hell are you doing? Quick, get something to wipe this off." Celeste held up the thin white sheet of drafting paper on which the brown coffee stains were rapidly soaking in. Little drips of coffee ran off the sheet onto the desk. Nick looked around wildly for some paper towels or napkins, but there wasn't anything in reach. Suddenly, he held up a hand. "I got it," he said. With one quick movement, he pulled his T-shirt off over his head, revealing his golden-tanned torso, and laid the drafting paper down on another desk, pressing the shirt against it at the same time. The coffee soaked rapidly into the soft cotton, spreading through the fabric and lifting off the paper. Celeste stared. Nick Saunders standing half naked in the Pinyon office cleaning up a spill had to be the very last thing she'd expected to see today. She realized her mouth was hanging open a little and shut it quickly.

After a minute, Nick held up the paper. "There," he said, surveying it critically. "That looks a little better." It was brown and wrinkly in spots, but all of the writing was legible.

There was a little silence. Nick grinned at Celeste as if he was waiting for her to say something. She looked down at the stained sketch. "Uh, thanks." More silence. "I, um, thought you were Travis."

"No, thank God." The muscles in his chest flexed as he perched on the edge of the desk. Celeste noticed that he had a smattering of golden freckles across his shoulders. "But you can pretend I'm Travis if it means I get more of that," he said.

"Don't start, Nick," she warned.

He widened his eyes innocently. "I just came down

here to get some work done, and now I'm being accused of something I haven't even done? Is this how you treat all your special Pinyon guests?"

Celeste started to respond and then paused. "Wait—what do you mean, get some work done?" She turned and eyed the pad of paper, untouched by spilled coffee. Scribbling in blue ink covered the first page.

Nick plopped down on a leather chair near the desk and propped his feet on the desk. He tipped back in the chair and laced his fingers behind his head. "For my screening party. Remember? The festival is coming up and this is my chance for some really big names to see my film. So I want the event to be the best one of the whole festival. "

Celeste glanced nervously at the door. Why hadn't Travis shown up by now? He was supposed to have been here ten minutes ago. She had a fleeting vision of her boyfriend bursting through the door, dressed up like Arnold Schwarzenegger in *Terminator*, and blasting Nick into a pulp with some giant futuristic rocket-launcher.

"Look, Nick, I'm sure your party is going to rock," she said. "But honestly, I'm not helping you. That's Devon's job. She's the guest relations rep. Sorry." She sat down at the desk and picked up a pencil, hoping he'd get the hint and leave.

Wishful thinking. Nick looked down at the scribbles

on his paper and played with a stapler for a minute. "Who's Devon?"

"The. Guest. Relations. Rep," Celeste said slowly, her patience waning. "And also my best friend. Trust me, she's awesome. And has plenty of party experience to draw from."

"I don't know." Nick looked up and dropped his feet to the floor. He leaned forward a little. "I was really looking forward to working with you." His voice dropped silkily.

Celeste grabbed her phone. This had to stop. "How about I call Devon right now? So you guys can get started?" Rapidly, she texted Devon. Luckily, Nick couldn't see the message, which read: HELP, MASSIVE FLIRT WANTS ME TO PLAN HIS PARTY, NEED YOU STAT. She pressed send and gave Nick a big smile, showing all of her teeth. "There. She should be here any minute."

The phone beeped and Celeste peered down at Devon's return message. SUPER-DEVON ON THE WAY. BTW MESSAGE FROM TRAVIS. BROKE A BELT ON THE MOWER, CAN'T COME OVER. Celeste exhaled. At least she didn't have to worry about a *Terminator* scene. She looked up at Nick. He was staring at her. Celeste looked away fast and then slid her eyes back. Still staring. Finally, she couldn't help herself.

"Why are you staring at me, Nick?" she snapped.

Nick shrugged and tapped a pen on the desk. There

was a little pause. The thought occurred to Celeste that she'd never actually been alone, like totally alone, with Nick for more than a few minutes. Well, except for those ill-advised hookup sessions last summer. The silence stretched out until it filled the room. Celeste wondered if he could hear her stomach rumbling and put her hand over her belly.

Then Nick put down the pen and leaned forward a little. "So, Celeste, what's your story?"

"What?" Celeste blinked rapidly.

"I mean, you and I have known each other for like five years or something, right?"

Celeste considered this. "Yeah, that's about right."

"Well, I can't figure out why you're still stuck here, working every summer. Did you commit some sort of crime at birth or something?"

Celeste bristled until she saw the playful crinkles around Nick's eyes. "Wait, what *am* I doing here?" she asked, going wide-eyed. "Oh my God! Rescue me, Nick Saunders!"

Nick laughed. "Funny. I never noticed that about you before. But seriously—why *do* they make you work here every summer?"

Celeste looked down at the now-dry seating plan. "It's not that I'm chained to the resort or something. It's just that . . ." She paused. "Well, my dad's really into the idea of the family working together—like really into it. I mean, this resort is my parents' entire life. I think if I told them I'd rather not work, they'd be really upset."

"So, you're destined to be towel-folder and drink-fetcher until college?" Nick smirked.

She shrugged. "I guess so. There was this program. . . ." She stopped. She wasn't about to tell Nick the Rich and Arrogant about her dream writing program just because he had managed to talk to her for twenty seconds without flirting. She looked down at the desk and made a little, insignificant mark on the seating chart.

"What program?" he asked.

She shook her head. "Nothing." Just then, the office door swung open and Devon walked in.

Celeste jumped up in relief. "Hey, Dev. Thanks for coming over."

Devon smiled. "No problem." She held her hand out to Nick. "I'm Devon Wright, the guest relations rep. I'm going to help you plan your party."

Nick took Devon's hand in his as though it were a precious offering. Now *his* mouth was hanging open. Celeste could hardly blame him. Devon was wearing a skin-tight white linen sheath dress, a string of giant blue beads that hung down practically to her waist, and a huge pink hibiscus tucked behind one ear.

As Celeste watched, Devon gave Nick a sexy little smile. "I'm going to make sure this is the best party ever," she purred.

Nick nodded dumbly, still hanging on to Devon's hand. "Great," he croaked. "That sounds great."

Celeste managed to stifle her snorting laughter in the crook of her forearm. Nick barely looked around as she crept from the room. Finally, Celeste felt like she'd found the one thing that could take Nick's mind off her—her best friend.

# Chapter Ten

◆

To Celeste, it seemed like Nick and Devon were everywhere she turned over the next couple of weeks. They were always walking around the resort, their heads together, talking and laughing. Sometimes, they seemed to actually be doing some party planning. Celeste saw Devon taking digital pictures of the pool area one day, while Nick suggested various angles. And it seemed like every time Celeste hung out with Devon, Devon's phone was ringing with another call from Nick.

She should be grateful, Celeste told herself. After all, she finally had Nick off her back. He was so wrapped up now that he had even stopped calling her with useless requests for Perrier at room temperature or six lemons on ice. Anyway, she didn't have time to think about the film festival. The resort was packed. Between Celeste's nonstop work and Devon's party planning, they'd barely had time to talk.

On yet another blisteringly hot day, Celeste was gathering up dirty glasses and scattered newspapers around the pool. The place was oddly deserted—it was too hot to sit outside, so most of the guests had retreated to their rooms to wait out the middle of the day. As she stooped to retrieve a crumpled *New Yorker* from under one of the chairs, Celeste wished that *she* were lying down on a soft duvet-covered bed somewhere, in a nice cool guesthouse, with the shades pulled down and the AC going full blast. She straightened up. The pool water glittered like a hard blue jewel in the blinding sun. She could feel the heat of the deck boards even through the rubber soles of her boat shoes.

Celeste heard footsteps behind her and turned around. Devon, looking beautiful and cool as usual in a pale yellow cotton sundress, with her black hair tied up at the back of her head, approached her. She was carrying two dripping cans of Diet Coke.

"You are an angel," Celeste said, accepting a frosty can and downing half of it in the first gulp. She collapsed onto a lounge chair. Devon perched on the edge of the next one and sipped her soda.

"I know. I could see you slaving away out here from the office window and had to rescue you."

"Thanks, babe." Celeste slurped again at her Diet Coke and wiped her forehead with her arm. "Were you working on party stuff?"

"Yeah. I was going over some photos of the pool area. Nick wants to have this tent over the water that makes it look like a ice castle—he saw it in *Vanity Fair*." Devon rolled her eyes. "I looked it up—it costs like five thousand dollars to rent!" Suddenly, she leaned forward conspiratorially. Celeste caught the look her on her face and started laughing.

"What? Is that your latest attempt at a spy face?"

Devon looked wounded. "Hey, I'm very stealth. Anyway, I was going to ask why you stopped hooking up with Nick? He's so gorgeous!"

Celeste rolled her eyes. "Because he went back to L.A. We've only ever been summer flirt buddies, and then, *briefly*, summer hookup buddies. Even before last summer, it's not like we were friends or anything. He's just a rich kid who enjoys annoying the staff of a resort his parents spend a lot of money at. Honestly, I'm just not into him *at all*. He's so obnoxious! Don't get me wrong—he's like the hottest guy I've ever seen, but we're *so* not right for each other. Plus, there's Travis."

Devon shrugged. "You *have* known Nick a lot longer than you've known Travis, so I guess it probably would've happened by now if it was meant to be."

Celeste stretched her tanned legs out in front of her

on the lounge chair and crossed her hands behind her head. "Ugh, I cannot believe we're having his conversation about Nick Saunders. I owe you one for keeping him out of my hair this summer. I'm pretty sure Travis would have a stroke if he saw Nick hanging around me like he usually does."

"No problem." Devon smiled. "I will *definitely* keep him out of your hair."

Celeste laughed. "Hey, did you hear about the staff party tomorrow night? It's going to rock—Dave knows this amazing spot. There are these hot springs way out in the middle of the desert. You need a jeep to get out there, but they're supposed to be awesome."

"I know!" Devon squealed. "The girls in the office told me about it. Is Travis going?"

"Yeah, of course—you know he never passes up an opportunity for free beer. We can drive over around nine. Travis is going to take his Wrangler."

"Oh, fun! It'll be just like that staff party in *Dirty Dancing*."

Celeste laughed. "Um, Dev, I think we need to talk about managing your expectations."

✦ ✦ ✦

The air was windy and warm when the girls piled into Travis's red Jeep Wrangler the next night. Strands of cloud whipped across the moon, which hung glowing in the black sky.

"This is going to be a killer party," Travis declared as Celeste climbed into the front seat and Devon folded herself into the back. "These springs are like fifteen miles out and there's like practically no road, just a track."

"I'm so excited!" Celeste squealed. "At last, freedom!" She flung her arms out the open window dramatically. "I feel like I've been paroled or something." She was feeling refreshed after a cool shower. She could tell Travis appreciated her choice of a ruffly white miniskirt by the way his eyes raked her legs when she swung into the front seat.

Travis gunned the motor and the car sped away down the curvy highway. The lights and noise of town faded behind them as the truck turned onto smaller and smaller paved roads and finally bumped onto a dirt path, heading out into the dark, silent night. Celeste rolled down the window and let the pinyon-scented air whip her face. It felt so good to be out of her everlasting uniform, just having fun, not worrying about her parents, or the resort, or anything.

After a little while, Travis slowed down.

"Is this it?" Celeste asked, craning her head. It just looked like more desert—piles of rocks, some sand, some rough grasses.

"Yeah, I think so," Travis answered. He pointed to a cluster of trucks parked by a dune and killed the engine.

With the headlights off, the full moon flooded the landscape, lighting everything in an eerie gray glow. It was so bright, Celeste could see the freckles on Devon's nose. All three of them stood by the truck for a minute, scanning around them.

"There they are!" Devon pointed to a group of figures about fifty feet away. The girls crunched over, picking their way around scattered red rocks and skirting clumps of tall desert grass. Celeste clutched Travis's arm and congratulated herself on wearing Tevas instead of flip-flops tonight.

As they approached, they could see a small campfire burning, with a few figures standing around it. Everyone else was sitting in a series of natural pools tucked in among the rocks. They looked like a lot of disembodied heads floating in the water. Steam wafted upward, concealing people's faces, and the rotten-egg smell of sulfur hung strong in the air.

"Hey, Celeste!" She turned at the sound of her name. Dave and Rick were waving from the other side of the fire. "Come here and give us a hug!"

Celeste trotted over. She could see that both of them had already been drinking for a while. Travis lumbered up behind her.

"This is an amazing party spot, Dave!" Celeste exclaimed. "Are all those pools, like, hot?"

"Yeah. The water comes up from underground and the pools just formed here. Some of them are really hot—like you'll boil yourself. This one's the best." He pointed to the largest pool where most people were sitting.

"So *why* am I just finding out about this place now?" Celeste demanded playfully.

Dave smiled and exchanged glances with Rick. A gold crown on one of his teeth caught the firelight and flashed. "Pinyon staff's been coming here forever, but you're a junior, right? We figured we didn't want to corrupt you *too* early." Everyone cracked up.

Celeste smacked Dave on the shoulder. "Well, I'm a big girl now, so you don't have to worry. In fact, you can get me a beer." She pointed to a big red cooler half buried in the sand.

Dave bent over and rummaged through the ice. "You girls want Miller Lite or Natty Light?"

"Um, Natty, I guess," Celeste said, and accepted a dripping cold bottle.

"I brought my own," Devon said.

"What?" Celeste turned to her friend.

Devon smiled wickedly and dug into her handbag to pull out a large silver flask. "I'm going classy tonight," she said, and twisted off the cap.

Celeste laughed. "You *are* going something—I'm not

sure *classy* is the word for it, though. Where'd you get the flask?"

Devon winked. "Where do you think?"

Celeste's eyes widened. *"Nick?"* she whispered so Travis wouldn't hear. Devon nodded.

"He said it's the *only* way to drink."

Travis draped his arm around Celeste's neck while he drained his beer. She gazed up at the huge bright moon. Suddenly, Travis's arm stiffened like cement around her shoulder and she felt his body go rigid. She looked up.

"What?" she asked. "What is it?" Travis didn't answer. He was staring across the sand at the cars. Celeste followed his gaze. There, sauntering casually toward them, swinging a six-pack from one hand and a bottle of vodka from the other, was Nick.

# Chapter Eleven

✦

No one else had noticed Nick's arrival. Travis clenched his fists. "What's *he* doing here?" he whispered gruffly.

Celeste could hardly hear him over the roaring in her ears. Bothering her at the resort was one thing, but harassing her off the grounds? What was his deal? Could he really still think that last summer mattered? Hadn't she made her not-available status perfectly clear?

Beside her, Travis made a rumbling noise in his throat and started forward, presumably to begin the work of pounding Nick's face into the sand. But Celeste shoved in front of him. She was going to have to deal with this herself.

She strode across the sand, her eyes fixed on Nick,

who was standing near the campfire, looking around. Searching for *me*, Celeste thought furiously. This was it. She was going to let him know that she did *not* appreciate all his obnoxious flirting this summer, she did not appreciate having to soothe her boyfriend constantly because of him, and most of all, she did *not* appreciate him following her here when she was trying to have a relaxing, fun night with her friends—she didn't care how rich and important his parents were!

Celeste drew closer to Nick. She clenched her hands into fists until her fingernails bit into her palms. She opened her mouth, but before she could say anything, she felt movement behind her. She turned and Devon brushed past, skimming across the sand like a moth.

"You came!" she cried, and threw herself on Nick's chest, almost knocking him over with the force of her hug. He staggered backwards a few steps. Celeste didn't move. What was going on?

Devon clutched at Nick's arm and beamed. "Isn't this place amazing?" she asked, staring up at his face worshipfully. Slowly, the realization of why Nick was here dawned on Celeste, who felt as if her mind were wading through mud. Devon had invited him. He was her date.

Nick smirked at Celeste as if he could read her mind. "Hey," he greeted her. "Thanks for letting me crash your party."

"Oh my God, it's totally no big deal!" Devon trilled

before Celeste could answer. "The more the merrier, right, Celeste?"

Celeste nodded dumbly. She trailed behind them as Devon steered Nick over to the fire and the beer coolers. Nick broke a beer off his six-pack and dumped the rest into the melting ice of the cooler. Celeste slipped back around the fire to Travis, who had obviously seen the whole thing. She wrapped her arm around his waist.

"He's here with Devon," she told him. "See? There's nothing to worry about."

Travis studied Devon and Nick, silhouetted by the fire, as they stood talking, and nodded slowly. "Good. I'm glad he's not here still trying to get on you."

"Of course not!" Celeste reassured him. She stared across the fire. Devon was gesticulating wildly as she talked. Celeste could hear her frequent laughter over the general chatter around them. Nick was nodding, his hand shoved in his pockets. He glanced at Celeste and caught her staring at them. He offered her a little smile and turned back to Devon.

Celeste tugged her arm free from Travis and sank slowly down on the sand to sit cross-legged. Travis wandered back over to the beer cooler. The sand felt cool under her legs and the fire was warm on her face. Idly, she gathered a few rocks from the sand and lined them up in front of her, turning the idea of Nick and Devon together over in her mind. She'd known Devon thought he was hot, but she hadn't known they were actually *together*—and hooking up, presumably. She snuck another glance at the pair across the fire. They were sitting down too, and Devon had her feet in Nick's lap, leaning back on her hands while she chattered away. Celeste couldn't hear what she was saying over the crackle of the fire, but Nick was laughing. Then Devon shoved Nick's shoulder. He clutched at her and fell over on the sand, pulling her with him. Travis suddenly reappeared from the beer cooler and thumped down on the sand beside Celeste. "There's no more Natty Light," he said, breathing heavily.

"Okay," she replied absently. Devon and Nick were whispering now, still lying on the sand. As Celeste watched, Devon tilted up the silver flask again and took another swig. Suddenly she jumped to her feet.

"Well, come on, you guys," she ordered Celeste and Travis. "Let's get in the water!" A lot of the other people who had been in the pools for a while were getting out and rubbing themselves with towels. Devon grabbed Celeste's hand and hauled her to her feet. "Come on!" she yelled. The boys stripped off their shirts and Devon shucked her tank top to reveal a very skimpy pink lace bra. They picked over the rocks toward the biggest pool. Celeste thought that it was a good thing she'd worn her black bra—it was almost like a bikini top.

"Dev," Celeste murmured as they balanced on the

wet red rocks around the pool, "that bra's going to be *totally* see-through once it gets wet."

Devon glanced down at her chest. "Oh yeah." Then she shot a sideways look at Nick, who was dipping a toe in the water. "Oh well!" she chirped. She touched a foot to the water and jerked it back. "It's hot!"

Celeste sat down on a rock and gingerly dropped her legs in. The sulfur-y gray water was almost too hot, but not quite. It was murky and dark. She wondered if there were any, say, biting fish that lived in the bottom of natural hot springs pools. She peered down at the water and suddenly something grabbed her ankle and pulled.

Celeste shrieked and bumped off the rocks, splashing awkwardly into the pool. The bottom was warm and sandy. She managed to stand up and spat some mineral water out. It tasted strongly of iron. Nick's blond head popped to the surface beside her. He grinned. "Sorry. Did I scare you? There aren't any sharks around here, you know."

Celeste rubbed her eyes. "You're an idiot, Nick," she said. She turned her back on him just as Travis splashed into the water next to her.

"Wow, this is really hot!" he said. Before Celeste could answer, Devon waded up. She had that trashed, glassy-eyed look Celeste recognized immediately.

"Hey, let's have a chicken fight!" Devon yelled, and

started trying to climb on Nick's back. She must have been pretty drunk though, because she slipped off and fell back into the water with a splash.

Nick rolled his eyes at Celeste and Travis and turned around to fish Devon out. "What do you think, Trav, can we handle them?" Nick asked.

Celeste winced automatically at Nick talking to Travis directly, but Travis didn't even seem to notice that his mortal enemy had presumed to address him.

"Awesome!" he said. "Me and Celeste against you and Devon." He slipped under the murky water, and Celeste suddenly felt herself rising in the air, perched precariously on his shoulders. She tipped one way and then the other and saved herself from falling off only by grabbing Travis's head.

"Ow! No death grips!" he yelled from beneath her.

Nick seemed to be having a little more trouble balancing Devon. She fell off several times before he managed to stand up with her. The boys walked slowly toward each other. Celeste and Devon screamed and grappled with each other's hands. Celeste was surprised to hear Nick and Travis fake-growling at each other and laughing. *Who would ever have thought Travis would be laughing with Nick?* she thought fleetingly, trying to grab one of Devon's slippery arms.

Nick slipped suddenly and fell, dumping Devon headfirst into the water with a massive splash. "We are the champions!" Celeste screamed. "Let me down, Travis."

"Oh no," he said and suddenly tipped forward. Celeste squealed as she tumbled from his shoulders and fell with a thump into his arms. Awkwardly, he clambered out of the pool, still holding her.

"Where are you taking me, big strong man?" Celeste giggled. She shivered as the cool night air brushed her still-steaming skin.

Travis leaned down and kissed her deeply as she wrapped her arms around his neck. "I'm going to take you back to the Jeep," he whispered huskily. "There's an old blanket in the back. We can spread it out under the stars—"

"And have a little alone time," Celeste finished. She reached up and kissed him again. His broad, warm chest felt so good against her body. She huddled close to him as he carried her over the rocks toward the cars.

"Mmm, that air smells so good," Travis said, inhaling deeply.

She took a deep breath of the clean, cold air. "It does. It smells amazing."

"Mmmm." Travis inhaled again. "Arrroo!" he suddenly howled at the sky like a coyote and started running, bumping Celeste over the rocky path.

"Hey!" she protested, laughing and hanging on to his neck. "If you drop me, you're dead, Travis."

"I won't drop you!" he shouted, running faster. The wind blew against Celeste's cheeks and she gripped his shoulders tighter.

"Okay, that's good, Travis!" she shouted. "Stop! You're going too fast." He didn't seem to hear her. Suddenly, near the cars, he stopped running and twirled around, whipping Celeste around with him.

"Okay, try this," he shouted. "Just look up at the sky while you're twirling. The stars look amazing."

"No, wait, Travis, don't twirl me, it makes me sick!" Celeste yelled, holding on tighter. The dark world of rocks and stars spun around her in a blur. "Put me down! Stop!"

Suddenly there was a *thunk* and Celeste felt her head connect with something hard. Travis stumbled and dropped her. "Ow!" Celeste cried as she landed on the sharp rocks.

"Shit, sorry," Travis said, sounding subdued. He kneeled beside her. Celeste could hear him breathing in the dark.

"Oooh, my head." Slowly, Celeste sat up, rubbing the back of her skull. "You ran me right into one of the cars, Travis. Nice going." She could feel a lump already rising up under her fingertips.

"Sorry," Travis repeated. He slid a hand under her elbow and tried to haul her to her feet.

"Stop!" Celeste snapped. "Just don't touch me,

okay?" She pulled herself up and carefully dusted off her wet, sandy rear. "Thanks for dropping me right on the rocks too." She turned and started heading back to the campfire, shivering as the wind caught her damp skin.

"I said I was sorry," Travis mumbled. "Hey, where are you going?"

"I'm going back to where it's warm," Celeste shot over her shoulder. "Sorry if I'm not feeling super-romantic right now."

Travis trotted to catch up with her. "Come on, Celeste, don't be mad."

"I'm not. I just don't appreciate having my head bashed into a car door, that's all." She walked faster and, reaching the warm orange ring of the campfire, sank down gratefully on the sand. Travis sat down next to her.

After a minute, she felt the touch of fleece and looked up as he wrapped his big hooded sweatshirt around her shoulders. He leaned forward and kissed her softly on the forehead.

"I'm really sorry," he said quietly. "I'm a moron sometimes."

"You are," she agreed, but his big stubbly face looked so pitiful that she softened and leaned against him. He pulled her into the crook of his arm. Devon and Nick staggered up panting and laughing, their clothes clinging to them. Devon flopped down on the sand. She took a deep breath and tried to wipe her face off with her sandy hands. Nick plopped down next to her.

"Whew!" he said. "That was awesome. Where's the beer?"

"Oh baby, we don't need beer," Devon giggled tipsily and leaned into Nick's lap. "Here, have some of this." She waved the silver flask in his face.

Nick pawed it away. "You're totally trashed, Devon," he told her. "I should cut you off."

"I'm not!" Devon giggled. "Whoops!" The silver flask slipped from her hand, tipping its precious contents into the sand. "Are you worried someone might try and take advantage of me, Nick?" She leaned over to whisper something. Celeste couldn't hear what she was saying but she could take an educated guess.

"Maybe later," Nick told Devon.

"Oh, but I–" The rest of Devon's words were lost as she murmured close to his ear. Nick glanced over at Celeste and Travis. Celeste couldn't believe it–he actually looked a little shocked. Amazing that Devon could actually make this wildly inappropriate jerk blush. She never would have thought it possible. "Um, okay," Nick told Devon. "See you guys later."

"Yeah! Have fun," Travis said. Celeste rolled her eyes and looked away.

"Come on!" Devon was on her feet, tugging at Nick's

hand. He got up and a grin split his face as he looked at Travis and Celeste.

"Don't wait up, kids!" he said. They disappeared into the darkness just beyond the ring of light cast by the campfire.

Travis laughed. "Maybe that guy's not as bad as I thought."

Celeste watched their retreating backs. Whatever. Nick could hang out with whomever he wanted. Now that she didn't have to worry about keeping Travis and Nick apart anymore, her summer had just gotten a lot easier, she thought. So why did she have a lump in her stomach?

# Chapter Twelve

◆

Several days after the beach party, Celeste was crouched, struggling to unlock the storage cupboard at the base of the towel station. Top on her list this morning was to refill the station, but when she finally got the sticky cupboard door open, she found an awful mess. The cupboard was a stew of jumbled-up towels, water bottles, and the sample tubes of sunscreen they were always handing out. Celeste sighed. She sat down cross-legged on the deck and started pulling everything out. The hot morning sun on her back and neck put her in a kind of trance as she steadily folded and stacked the eighty thousand white Pinyon towels. Only a few guests were out by the pool, and a sense of peace and quiet lay over the place. The only sounds were the dry rustle of the palmetto fronds overhead and the gentle splashing of the turquoise pool water as a sleek, dark-haired woman stroked from one side of the pool to the other, over and over.

"Hey," a voice said from behind her. Celeste turned her head around so fast she could hear her neck crack. Nick sank onto a lounge chair next to her and stretched his legs out in front of him and his arms over his head. "Ahh," he said, letting out his breath. "This is nice."

Celeste resumed her folding. "I haven't seen you around for the last few days," she said, watching her hands instead of his face. "I thought maybe you'd gotten bored of the country life and hitched back to L.A. or something," she teased.

Nick grinned without opening his eyes. "Nah. I'm starting to actually like it here."

"Wow. Thanks for the glowing compliment." Celeste smacked him with a towel.

"Hey! No abusing the guests. Devon and I have been doing a ton of work on the screening party. We still don't have a theme though." He looked around suddenly, as if something had occurred to him. "Where's your Neanderthal boyfriend?" he asked.

"Dude, I thought you guys were getting along." Celeste piled the first stack of folded towels into a corner of the storage cupboard.

"Oh, we are. Just as long as he understands that I like

my face arranged just how it is." Nick dropped his head back on the lounge and closed his eyes.

"So why don't you have a theme yet?" Celeste asked. "Are you and Devon too busy exploring each other's *minds*?" She grinned at him, getting to her feet and lining the water bottles up in a neat row on the top of the towel station. The sun was beating down on the back of her neck and she lifted her hair up. She looked around and caught Nick staring at her. He dropped his gaze fast and tucked his hands behind his head again.

"I don't know—we've tossed around a million ideas. Doing a color theme—like the Truman Capote Black and White Ball. Or maybe something with a jungle theme. I kind of like that—you know, tigers strolling around, bird noises over the speakers."

Celeste considered this. "I don't know if that would give the party the right . . ." She searched around for the word. ". . . *ambiance*—you know what I mean?"

Nick nodded. He swung his legs around the side of the chair and planted his feet on the deck. "Hey, toss me a water bottle, would you?"

Celeste flipped one of the cool clear bottles over to him and he caught it in one hand. He unscrewed the top, took a long drink, and then stopped. He held up the bottle and examined it.

"What?" Celeste asked.

"Hey," he said slowly. "What about a water theme?

Everything water . . . like all blue and white and transparent things."

Celeste thought for a minute and then nodded. "I think that could work. You mean like see-through blue fabric, maybe, and, like, fancy waters all laid out somewhere?"

"Yeah!" Nick said, leaping to his feet. "And we could get one of those clear dance floors that goes over the pool water."

"That would be awesome." Celeste was catching some of his excitement.

"Yeah, everyone would be, like, walking on water." Nick reached out and grabbed Celeste around the waist, twirling her dangerously close to the pool.

She gasped. His face seemed very close above hers and his arms were tight around her waist. She giggled. All of a sudden, her feet left the ground as he swept her up and tipped her backwards in an exaggerated dip. "Nick!" she yelled, still laughing. She faux-struggled to release herself and took a clumsy swing at his shoulder. He pulled her in tighter.

"Ow! Is this how you always treat your dance partners?" He grinned, swinging her back up as if she weighed nothing at all and setting her on her feet. His arm stayed around her waist, and she felt his breath on her face. His teeth flashed very white against his tanned skin.

Suddenly, Celeste saw a blur of white polo shirt out of the corner of her eye and just managed to yell, "Trav–" before the blur hit Nick across the back with blinding force.

Nick let out a startled "ooof" and staggered before catching his balance. He straightened up just in time to catch Travis's fist landing on his jaw. He reeled backwards, crashing into a lounge chair.

"Travis, stop!" Celeste screamed, catching at her boyfriend's arm, which felt like a bar of steel under her hands.

Travis didn't even look around. "I'm sick of this slime following you around and hitting on you all the time," he yelled, his face red and shiny. "It's ridiculous. He needs to go back to *L.A.*, where he belongs."

By now, Nick had gotten to his feet and was standing in front of Travis, breathing heavily, his cheek showing the bright red mark of Travis's fist. "Whatever, Celeste," he said tightly, his eyes fixed on Travis. "If he wants to think I was hitting on you, then fine. Let's do it. Let's get all this out right now." He clenched his hands.

Travis turned and rushed Nick. The two fell to the deck, grappling with each other.

"Stop! Stop right now!" Celeste screamed. "This is stupid!"

Neither of them paid the least attention. They rolled over on the deck, dangerously near the edge of the pool, and Celeste saw Nick sock Travis in the eye before Travis grabbed Nick and rolled over again so that he was on top. Celeste could see what was about to happen. "No, Travis!" she screamed.

He didn't even seem to hear her. He drew his fist back.

"What the *hell* is going on here?" a voice roared from behind Celeste.

Celeste's dad stood at the pool gate, his hands on his hips and his eyes blazing. Startled, Travis sent his punch awry, bouncing off Nick's shoulder instead of his face. Nick saw Travis's attention distracted and seized his chance. He threw his weight upward and grabbed Travis's shirt, ripping it down the front. The two rolled over again—right into the pool.

A huge splash soaked Mr. Tippen, the deck, and part of Celeste's shirt. Travis and Nick surfaced immediately, staggering to regain their balance in the shallow end. Their hair was plastered to their heads, and Travis's shirt was torn away from the collar, hanging around his neck by a few shreds like a ridiculous halter top. Nick's cheek was already swelling up, making one half of his face look distinctly chipmunky.

Celeste realized that she was still clutching an armload of folded towels. Shaking a little, she carefully set them down on top of the towel station, smoothing them out and lining up the edges, just as she had always been taught. She cast a furtive glance at the other guests and cringed. Everyone had put down their newspapers and magazines and was staring in horror and fascination. The dark-haired swimmer had stopped her laps. As Celeste watched, the woman cast the boys a disdainful glance. Then she climbed delicately from the pool and turned her back on the group, padding to the opposite end of the deck. Damn. This could be bad. Nothing like a good old bar brawl to really lend an air of class to the place.

Mr. Tippen stood at the edge of the pool, his hands on his hips. He stared down at the boys with a gaze that could have fried an egg. For a moment that lasted about twenty years, he just stared in silence. Then he spoke.

"Nick, I certainly will expect proper behavior from you this summer as a guest at Pinyon. Don't let this sort of thing happen again. Travis and Celeste, I'll see you both in my office in ten minutes." With that, he spun on his heel and disappeared out the gate.

Not looking at the two boys, Celeste collapsed slowly onto a lounge chair and rested her head on her knees. She must have been on crack earlier when she'd been thinking that everything might actually work out this summer—that Nick would behave himself, that Travis and Nick wouldn't rip each other's arms off, that her dad would actually see that Travis wasn't the moron he thought. Celeste cradled her head in her arms. Yeah. Definitely not the summer she'd imagined.

# Chapter Thirteen

✦

For a minute, no one spoke. Celeste stared at the towels on the towel station. Then, with a giant heave, Nick climbed out of the pool. His white shirt clung to his chest and back, and his shorts hung heavy and dark with water. "Well, that was fun," he said. "Maybe we can do again it sometime. See you around, Celeste," he said, and sloshed away, leaving a line of puddles behind him.

Celeste whirled around to face Travis, who was still standing in the waist-deep water. "What the hell were you doing?" she hissed. "Get out of the stupid pool—you look like an idiot."

Travis climbed from the water obediently. "Sorry about that, babe," he said, looking down at his ruined T-shirt.

*"Yeah,"* Celeste said. "You should be. Now you're in huge trouble with my dad."

"But he was hitting on you," Travis pleaded, taking a step toward Celeste. She stepped back.

"Don't touch me—you're all wet. And he wasn't hitting on me. He was talking about dancing for his party. It was what us grownups call a *conversation.* You'll notice that I still have all my clothes on and that, even if he was hitting on me, I'm not exactly just going to start accidentally making out with him. A little trust might be nice."

"But—"

"Whatever." Celeste turned away disgustedly. "We better get over to the office. My dad's waiting for you."

They gathered quite a few curious glances from guests as they headed toward the office, but Celeste was too upset to care. *How could Travis do this?* she thought furiously. Once again, he'd proven that he had no idea that his actions actually had consequences—for her or her family. He just did whatever he wanted all the time. The effect on her never entered his mind. Celeste cast a sidelong glance at her boyfriend as they walked along. His eye was swelling up and there was a long red mark across one cheek. *He even looks like a thug,* she thought bitterly.

Travis pushed open the door of her dad's office and the blast of air-conditioning hit them. Celeste shivered and followed him in.

Her dad was tapping on the computer and didn't

look up. "Sit down," he said, waving his hand in Travis's direction. Travis sank onto a plastic and metal chair while Celeste nestled herself in a corner of the ugly, nubby plaid sofa and tried to be invisible.

Mr. Tippen finished what he was typing and leaned back in his chair. He tapped a pen on his desk. Travis unconsciously straightened his back and clasped his hands between his knees like a little boy waiting to be called on in school.

"Well, Mr. Helding," Dad said. "It seems to me that you are one strike away from losing your job."

Celeste started up from the sofa and opened her mouth to protest, but her father glared at her and she fell back in silence.

"Strike one, of course, was forfeited by stealing the golf cart in the first place. And, as I observed by the pool, you've just used up strike two. That would leave one more strike and you're gone from Pinyon." Mr. Tippen's voice rose slightly at the end of his last sentence and his grip on his pen tightened.

Travis nodded. "Mr. Tippen–" he began.

Celeste's dad cut him off. "I am not finished speaking, Travis. Now, I recall that at the beginning of the summer I had a long conversation with your parents. And they made it perfectly clear to me that this debacle was to be entirely your responsibility. If you lose your job at Pinyon because of your own immaturity, you will be responsible for the rest of the golf cart damages yourself. And let me tell you, the value of golf cart is significantly higher than what an eighteen-year-old can earn in a single summer. I don't think you'll want to be burdened with that, do you?"

"No, sir," Travis mumbled, staring down at his knees.

"Good." Mr. Tippen stood up and Celeste couldn't help thinking that he had really missed his calling when he went into resort management. He definitely should have been a high school principal instead. "Then I trust there will be no more problems like this." His voice was frosty.

"Yes, sir," Travis said again, like a parrot.

"And Celeste." Her father turned his gaze on her and she cringed involuntarily. "I don't know what part you had in all of this, and to be perfectly honest, I'd rather not know."

Celeste forced herself to keep looking him in the face. It wasn't easy, since it felt like his eyes were boring holes in her head.

"All I can do is remind you—again—that this family depends on the success of the resort, and that success depends on the happiness of our guests." He leaned across the table and skewered her with another stare. "Including the Saunders family. See that you keep that in mind."

Celeste gulped and nodded. Her father waved his hand at them dismissively and turned back to his desk.

Travis got up and shambled toward the door, Celeste trailing in his wake. She looked back at her father. He was already typing again on the computer. A quiet exit seemed like the best strategy.

Out on the pathway, Celeste turned to Travis, her hands on her hips. His halter top/ripped shirt had dried somewhat but still looked totally stupid. "Look, Travis, we have to talk," she said.

He sighed noisily. "Don't you think I've been bawled out enough for one day? I said I was sorry, remember? What do you want me to do, stab myself with hot needles? The little punk deserved it anyway."

A guest in a bathrobe was coming down the path. Celeste grabbed Travis's arm and dragged him off to the side, behind a clump of azalea bushes. Stiff twigs poked her in the back. "Look," she hissed. "Whatever I have to say, you deserve it. Your stupid temper got me in trouble, pissed off my dad, and possibly screwed up our family business. You heard my dad in there—it's my *job* to laugh at Nick's stupid jokes and listen to his stories. The Saunderses are our *customers*! Keeping them happy keeps *us* in business. So if you beat up their son, that makes them unhappy, get it?"

A sulky look crossed Travis's face. He crossed his arms over his chest. "Hey, listen, Ms. Pissy 2009, maybe you should be happy that I was *trying* to defend your honor. I mean, the guy was pawing you all over!"

Celeste felt the blood rise in her temples and couldn't resist actually stamping her foot. "Travis! You are so irritating! First of all, number one, Nick was not hitting on me, for the billionth time. He was talking about his party. And two"—she waved her fingers in his face—"that little piece of class down there in the pool was *not* about me or my honor. It was all about being a stupid guy and doing some sort of marking-your-territory thing, like some dog peeing on a fence. I am *not* your fence, Travis Helding, so don't think you need to get all badass for me." She stopped and took a deep breath. Her head was pounding. Travis opened his mouth as if to say something.

"Shut up! I'm not done. Furthermore, it's revolting that you think I actually *need* defending. I mean, wouldn't you trust me to shut Nick down if he was really hitting on me?"

Travis stood still a minute, his mouth hanging open. "Okay, fine," he said carefully, as if talking to a dangerously deranged person. "Look, I'll try not to let that little Saunders prick get under my skin, okay?" He laid a tentative hand on her arm.

Celeste took a deep breath. "Look, I'm sorry I'm freaking out, but all I want is for us to have a good summer together. I really, really want to drive up to Tempe with you to help you move into school, and if you screw up, there's no way my dad will let me. So just ignore Nick, okay? The summer's almost half over anyway."

Travis nodded slowly. "Okay, babe. I'll do my best—after all, I get to spend the summer with you, right?"

Celeste let him hug her. "Thanks," she said. Travis turned and pushed out of the bushes. But as she watched him trudge up the path, she had a feeling that the Travis-Nick saga was far from over.

# Chapter Fourteen

✦

Celeste!" Devon's shrill voice zinged into Celeste's ear. The door to her bedroom banged open, smacking the wall, and Devon bounded in. "Are you awake? Listen to this!" She plopped down on the side of Celeste's bed.

Celeste peeked one eye out of the covers. The room was golden with morning sunlight, and dust motes danced in a ray of sun across her bed. She groaned and squinted at the clock. "Devon, why are you here at"—she squinted again—"seven o'clock? Are you out of your mind?" She pulled the old quilt back over her head and closed her eyes. Devon jerked down the quilt. "Listen to this! Are you ready?"

"Do I have any choice?"

"Shut up! Just listen." Devon cleared her throat and tossed her hair over one shoulder. "'Dear Ms. Wright.'" She paused to take a self-referential bow. "That's me. 'Dear Ms. Wright. We are delighted to inform you that we have had an opening in the Thistlebottom School Summer Thespian Program in Aberdeen, Scotland. As you are first on the waiting list, we would like to offer you the spot. Please bring with you a passport, other photo identification, and a good wool sweater, as Aberdeen can be chilly even in the summer. We will expect your confirmation answer shortly. Sincerely, John MacArthur, Dean, Thistlebottom School Summer Thespian Program.'"

Celeste looked down, fiddling with the quilt for a minute as she tried to swallow the lump that had suddenly risen in her throat. It would've been really nice to get a letter like that from the Berkshires program. But who was she kidding? She wouldn't have been able to accept it anyway. Celeste looked up. Devon was watching her expectantly. She swallowed hard and mustered an approximation of a happy smile.

"That's awesome!" Celeste cried, throwing her arms around her best friend. "Scotland will be so amazing. You're going to come back even more of a drama queen than you are now. When do you leave?"

Devon hesitated. "Well, I talked to the program secretary this morning and they want me there by Thursday."

Celeste's jaw dropped. "Wait, you mean *this* Thursday? Today's Tuesday!"

Devon nodded. "I know. So I booked a flight to London that leaves tomorrow morning. I'll spend the night there and then fly to Scotland the next day." She looked up and did her best conflicted-emotions squint. "I feel horrible leaving you here!" she whispered.

It *would* be hard facing the entire rest of the summer without Devon. She reminded herself that that was her problem, though, not Devon's. If it was *her* going to the Berkshires, she'd want Devon to be happy for her, not make her feel guilty.

Celeste hugged her friend again. "Oh my God, I'll be totally fine! You'll meet tons of yummy Scottish guys, and when you come back, we'll have so much gossip to catch up on. And you have to bring me something amazing from Scotland as a present." She lay back in bed and pulled the covers up again.

Devon screwed up her face, thinking. "Like something plaid?"

"Yeah. I guess they have a lot of that there," Celeste agreed, rearranging her pillows under her head. "Plaid and . . . sheep, right?"

"Right. And wool scarves." Devon picked one of Celeste's bras off the floor and wrapped it around her neck like a muffler.

"That's a nice look on you." Celeste laughed. "Okay,

so maybe we'll skip the present," she said. "But you have to promise me not to feel guilty. Then I'll just feel bad too."

"I promise," Devon pledged, bouncing off the bed. "Okay, so I have to go talk to your dad. Oh, and Nick."

Celeste opened her mouth to ask why Devon had to talk to Nick, when she realized what her friend was saying. "Right, Nick," she said slowly. "I forgot about that. You guys have been party planning nonstop, huh?"

"Yeah, we have." Devon paused with her hand on the doorknob. "I guess you'll be in charge of that now."

"I guess so," Celeste said, her mind whirling. Now she'd just have to explain to Travis that she'd be working with Nick, like, every day, for the rest of the summer. No problem.

"Don't worry," Devon assured her. "I'm totally organized—I've got everything we've done so far in this big binder, with a list of all the stuff that needs to be done, and all the people we've talked to. It'll be a breeze." She banged out the door. Celeste could hear her start the "What's in a name?" monologue from *Romeo and Juliet* on her way down the hall.

Celeste scrubbed her face with her hands and tried to organize her thoughts. Okay. Working with Nick. It wouldn't be so bad. True, he still tried to flirt with her at every available opportunity and didn't seem to understand the potential he had to ruin her life, but they'd had a couple of good conversations too—enough for her to see that he was actually capable of treating her like a human being.

Celeste threw back the covers and picked her way around her clothes-strewn floor to the bathroom. She turned on the shower and stared idly in the mirror as she waited for the water to heat up. And Travis. He might be okay too. He'd been on his best behavior ever since the fight with Nick. Maybe if she just explained to him again that her relationship with Nick was strictly business and that she had no choice in planning the party, he'd just relax and chill out, like he should have been doing all along.

With these comforting thoughts firmly in place, Celeste pulled off her tank top and boy shorts and stepped into the steaming shower, letting the water drum on top of her long hair and fall over her face. She'd go talk to Nick as soon as she was dressed.

✦ ✦ ✦

Celeste banged out of the house and headed for the Saunders villa. She wanted to talk to Nick about the situation before he heard it from someone else—and got any ideas about what this meant for their "relationship." Outside, the morning was fresh and a little dewy with that crisp air you find only in the desert. The resort sparkled like a jewel, waiting for the day to begin. The pool lay still and smooth as glass, and a crisp white towel lay on every chaise lounge, which were lined up in perfect rows around the pool. Inside the lobby, Celeste could see the floors still glistening from mopping. A housekeeper was placing vases of fresh lilies on the reception and concierge desks.

But Celeste barely noticed any of this. She was so intent on her mission that she didn't even notice her father coming toward her on the path.

"Oof!" Mr. Tippen said, as Celeste barreled right into him. "Good morning to you too."

Celeste straightened up. "Sorry, Daddy. Hi. Good morning."

"I was just coming to find you. I have to talk with you, Celeste," her father said.

Celeste groaned inwardly. She really wanted to talk to Nick as soon as she could, but she couldn't really say that to her father. "Okay, Dad," she responded meekly and followed him to his office.

Her father sank into his creaky leather chair and leaned forward on the peeling laminate desk. Celeste plopped down in her usual place in the corner of the plaid sofa. She pulled one of the throw pillows onto her lap and tucked her legs underneath her.

"Devon told me that she's leaving for Scotland tomorrow morning," Dad said.

Celeste nodded. "I know. She woke me up at the crack of dawn to tell me the news."

"So that leaves us with the problem of who will take over the planning for the Saunders party. Now, Maria is going on maternity leave any day. We can't depend on her to take over a major project right now. Simon is tied up with the Hargrove wedding. Your mother and I are going to be overseeing the entire festival—we can't take the time to focus on only one event. So that leaves you, Celeste."

Celeste nodded. "No problem. In fact, I was just on my way over to talk to Nick about the party."

Her father leaned forward and clasped his hands, his craggy face serious. He was tanned red-brown from the sun, but the lines around his eyes were white from squinting. "I know I don't need to remind you what happened the other day at the pool, Celeste."

She gulped. She'd thought maybe the whole Travis-Nick mess could fade quietly into the background. Obviously, she'd thought wrong. Her father went on.

"Your boyfriend has put the family in a potentially tenuous position with regard to our guests."

Celeste opened her mouth to protest, but her father glared at her.

"I should have fired him, but I didn't," he said, his voice rising slightly. "So what I need from you, Celeste, is even more commitment to making this festival, and the Saunders party, truly memorable. It's your duty to the family." Dad suddenly cracked a smile. "I wouldn't give you this kind of responsibility if I didn't think you could handle it. You're a smart girl, Celeste, and a hard worker."

"Thanks, Dad," she replied, breathing a little easier. Making the party a success—she could do that.

Dad shuffled through some papers on his desk and chose a printout of an Excel spreadsheet. "This is a big deal, Celeste," he said. He ran his finger down a column. "We're booked to capacity for that weekend—all with film-festival attendees. And these aren't just any guests. A group from Miramax has taken three guesthouses. The studio head of Searchlight is coming in and bringing several top directors."

"Wow," Celeste said, honestly impressed. She'd known Mr. and Mrs. Saunders were successful, but she'd had no idea they had so much influence.

"Wow is right," her father replied. "We want these people to love Pinyon. If they have a good time, they'll tell their friends. It'll be like building a billboard in L.A.—but without bankrupting us."

"That's awesome, Dad." She knew how much this meant to him—to her whole family. Even though they'd always been successful, her dad had been waiting for this kind of publicity for the resort for years.

"So, we need to make this festival the best event the resort has ever seen. If you're going to be in charge of one of the showpiece parties, I'm counting on you to plan the highlight of the festival." He fixed her with a piercing gaze. "Do you understand?"

Celeste straightened up. This was her chance to really impress her father. All the mess with Nick and Travis, all his doubts about her judgment in choosing Travis as her boyfriend—she could erase all of that by making the Saunders party unforgettable. She'd be on her way to help Travis move into the dorms in Tempe at the end of summer with no problem. And maybe, just maybe, if he was really impressed, he'd let her go to the Berkshires next summer instead of working. Her heart leaped at the thought. "Dad," she said in her most mature voice, "I'm going to work incredibly hard on this party, and when I'm done, I swear, it will be amazing. You don't have to worry about a thing."

Her father smiled. "Good. I'm glad to hear you taking this so seriously. I have a lot of confidence in you, Celeste."

She sprang up from the sofa. "Okay, well, I better go get started, right?" Dad nodded as she slipped from the room, her heart beating fast in anticipation. She could do this—after all, hadn't she had six summers of practice? This was going to be the most amazing party Pinyon had ever seen, Celeste thought. As long as she could keep her cohost and her boyfriend from killing one another until after the guests left, of course.

# Chapter Fifteen

✦

As she approached the Saunders guesthouse, Celeste saw the front door open and Mr. and Mrs. Saunders emerge, carrying towels. They both were wearing huge sunglasses, and Mrs. Saunders was teetering along on a pair of three-inch platform espadrilles. Before they could see her, Celeste ducked behind a storage shed at the side of the path. She just really didn't want to get waylaid by another "And how is your summer going, Celeste?" small-talk conversation, like she always got sucked into with guests. They had a tendency to drag on for a long, long time, and she was on a mission.

The Saunderses passed her hiding place, so close that Celeste could smell Mrs. Saunders's sunscreen. When they were safely past, she slipped out and ran to the back door of the guesthouse. The glass doors stood open but the screens were closed. Celeste stood for a minute, wondering whether she should knock or something, but Nick was probably still sleeping. After all, wasn't sleeping all morning standard rich jerk behavior? Finally, she just slid back the screen and stepped into the spacious kitchen.

Nick was standing at the counter, wearing nothing but a pair of baggy gray gym shorts and drinking a glass of orange juice. His hair stood up in sleep-tangled whorls, and his eyes had only made it about halfway open.

"Oh, sorry!" Celeste said. "Uh, the door was open." She could feel her face turning red. For some reason, seeing him when he'd clearly just woken up was like walking in on him in the shower or something. "I'll come back later," she stammered and felt for the door latch behind her.

"Hey, why are you leaving?" Nick asked, calmly finishing his juice. He didn't seem the least surprised to see her in his kitchen. "What's up?"

"Oh, um, nothing," Celeste said. Why was she still acting like an idiot? *Come on, Celeste*, she told herself sternly. *He's wearing gym shorts. Get a grip!* She shook her head. "Actually, yeah, there is something. Have you talked to Devon yet?"

Nick shook his head. "No. Why?"

"Well, she got into that acting program she wanted to go to in Scotland. And she's leaving tomorrow morning for the rest of the summer." Celeste looked down at her worn boat shoes.

"Ohhh," Nick said.

"So," Celeste said continued. "I guess—"

"Do you want to go get some breakfast?" Nick asked abruptly. He turned and started heading out of the room.

"Well, um," Celeste stammered. "I just wanted to tell you that—"

Nick was heading down the hall. "There've got to be some places in town, right? I've barely been out of the resort since we got here. I'll just put on some clothes. . . ." His voice trailed away and Celeste could hear a distant door slam.

She stood in the center of the entryway, in the perfect silence of the airy guesthouse. This wasn't really going like she'd expected. Nick didn't even seem concerned that Devon was gone. She had to make him understand how important this party was—and that their relationship was going to stay strictly business. A checklist of all the things she needed to do today whirled through her head until Nick reappeared in jeans and a worn gray T-shirt. He slapped his back pocket to check for his wallet.

"Ready?" he asked Celeste, pulling a set of car keys from his pocket.

"Um." She looked at her watch. "I'm not technically

on duty until noon, but I probably should check the—"
She didn't finish her sentence. Nick was already out the
door, heading down the path to an Alfa Romeo coupe
parked in the driveway.

"Wow," Celeste said, momentarily diverted. "Where'd
you get this car? I thought you guys had a Mercedes."

Nick slid into the driver's seat and leaned across to
open the passenger door for Celeste. "We do, but my
dad was getting tired of it. He had this baby driven up
from L.A. the other day. Nice, huh?" He turned the key
in the ignition and listened appreciatively to the roar of
the engine.

"Yeah." Celeste climbed in. "So, Mary's Food Shack
in Red Dunes is good for breakfast. They've got eggs
and bacon and stuff. The town's like five miles from
here or so."

"Awesome." Nick threw the car into gear and floored
the accelerator. Outside the gates, he turned onto the
two-lane road that ran from the resort into town and
punched the radio. "Free Fallin'" by Tom Petty came on.
Celeste rolled down her window and let the wind blow
through her hair. It felt great to be zipping along like
this, encased in buttery soft leather, instead of folding
endless towels in the sun or fetching lemon water and
carrying yoga mats for the rarely appreciative guests.

"And I'm free . . . free fallin' . . ." Tom cried on the
radio.

"I love this song!" Nick shouted over the wind whipping through the car. Celeste couldn't help grinning.

"Me too," she confessed. "Tom Petty was actually one of my first concerts."

"No way!" Nick glanced over. "I saw him in San Francisco once."

Wow. An actual conversation with Nick Saunders. Weird. "The café's up here on the right," Celeste told him as they entered Red Dunes and slowed down a bit. She pointed to a little yellow building on the main street. Nick pulled into a parking space next to an aqua blue Toyota Prius. Even though Red Dunes was only a few miles from Palm Springs, it was still small and sleepy enough to have slant parking on Main Street. The tourists spent all their time at the resorts just outside of town. It was mostly just locals who came around here.

"They have amazing bacon," Celeste said as they pushed through the glass door and into the steamy interior of Mary's. The heavenly smell of frying grease and coffee hit them full in the face. The place was crowded with people from town and various resort employees but they managed to nab a booth by the window.

Celeste slid across the slick red leather seat and grabbed the hem of her white skirt as it rode up on her thighs, practically flashing her nude-colored bikini to the whole restaurant. Quickly, she glanced at her breakfast companion, but he didn't even seem to have noticed. He was busy studying the one-page menu encased in limp plastic. It was a little weird, Celeste thought, being out like this with him. There had been no flirting since they left the resort, just basic friendliness.

"Hi there."

Nick and Celeste looked up. A plump, gray-haired waitress with a stained white apron around her ample middle was standing over them, her pen poised. "What can I get you?"

"I'll have the oatmeal with strawberries and a side of bacon, please," Celeste said. "And a coffee."

"I'll have the three-egg breakfast, scrambled, with home fries, toast, a double order of bacon, a short stack of pancakes, and the fruit bowl. And a large orange juice and a large coffee." Nick smiled pleasantly and handed back the menu. "Thanks."

Celeste was staring at him with her mouth open. "Nice breakfast," she said. Nick shrugged.

"I'm always starving. I probably have a tapeworm or something."

Celeste took a deep breath. "Okay, look, Nick, we have to talk."

He arranged his face in an innocent expression and folded his hands like a little boy in school. "What ith it, Mithith Tippen?" he asked in a lisp.

"Be serious—this is important. Devon's leaving," she began.

"Right," he said.

"So, my dad wants"—Celeste hesitated—"*me* to be in charge of planning the screening party with you. Like figuring out the theme, hiring the vendors and the band, getting the stuff for the film showing in place, doing the publicity—everything." She watched him carefully. His face remained totally blank and neutral. She went on. "And this party is going to be a really big deal—like huge. I mean, the whole festival is a big deal. This is really our chance to show the guests what Pinyon can do."

Nick nodded. "I get it. I mean, I want this to be perfect as much as you do—if my film gets a good reception, who knows what could happen? Maybe it would even get picked up. . . ." His face turned red and he looked down at his hands and fidgeted with a paper napkin.

Celeste raised her eyebrows. This was the first time she'd actually seen the suave and cool Nick actually look, sort of, well, unsure.

Nick looked up from the napkin, which he had impaled on the tines of his fork. "So all this is actually just me being selfish. And you can always count on me to pull through with *that*, right?" His old devilish grin flashed across his face, and he sat back, draping one arm over the back of the booth and stretching his legs out under the table.

"Here you go." The waitress set down their food.

Celeste stirred her oatmeal and watched Nick stuff half his eggs into his mouth in the first bite.

"So, what's the deal with your movie, anyway?" Celeste asked, pouring milk over the oatmeal so that it swirled with the brown sugar on top. "I mean, don't you spend all your time hanging out with the Olsen twins and Rumer Willis at clubs?" she teased. "When did you find time to do actual work?"

Nick laid several strips of bacon on top of his toast, which he'd slathered in butter and jelly, and put another piece of toast on top. He looked at the whole thing with satisfaction and took a huge bite. "Ashfter . . ." he tried to say, spraying a few crumbs across the table. He held up a finger. Celeste waited while he chewed. He tried again. "After I finished the film for my film studies class, I thought it could be better if I took more time with it." He shrugged. "So I got permission to use the editing studio at UCLA and worked on it a bunch this year."

"Yeah?" Celeste said, spooning up some oatmeal. "Most people wouldn't work on something after it was due, if it was for a class."

Nick shrugged. "Well, it was *my* project. I wanted it to be good." He took another gargantuan bite of his toast-and-bacon sandwich.

"Yeah, I totally know what you mean," Celeste said, a little more enthusiastically than she'd intended. Nick looked up, surprised.

Celeste focused on her oatmeal bowl instead of meeting his eyes. The words had just slipped out.

"What do you mean? Do you have a film too?" Nick asked.

Celeste could feel her face getting hot. She stirred her coffee a little too hard, slopping some out onto the table. "Um, no, not a film or anything. It's just that I did that once with a story," she mumbled, laying her napkin over the coffee spill and watching the brown liquid spread across the white paper.

Nick looked interested. "What are you, a writer or something?"

Celeste looked at the ceiling and then out the window, hoping that if she just ignored the question, he would forget about it and they could move on to another subject. But when she looked back at Nick, he was still waiting for an answer. She dropped her eyes to her plate and nibbled at a strip of bacon.

"I'm not really," she said. "I just like to write stories and stuff sometimes. Just for myself."

"So wouldn't that make you a writer then?" Nick asked.

"No, definitely not. I mean, it's not like I'm *good* or anything."

Nick picked up his fork and stabbed the stack of pancakes. "Usually the people who say they're awesome writers suck and people like you turn out to be the *real* writers," he remarked, sawing off a hunk of syrup-soaked pancake. "Anyway, what do you mean, you did something like that with a story once?"

Celeste shook her head. "It was nothing. Just that I really liked this story I wrote for English, so I kept working on it later—for almost the whole rest of the year."

"Cool," Nick said. "Can I read it sometime?"

"No!" Celeste almost shouted. "I mean, um, no thanks. I'm not really used to showing my writing to anyone. Anyway, can we please talk about the party? We have to get focused." She pulled out a notebook she'd slipped into her bag earlier that morning and flipped to a clean page. "Okay, so what have you and Devon done so far?"

Nick shoved his empty plate aside and laced his fingers behind his head. "Well, we've decided it should be at the pool."

"Okay, that's a start." Celeste wrote that down in her notebook.

"And remember when we were talking about making the theme 'water'? Well, I think we should stick with that. I think that would be awesome, especially since the film has a lot of water motifs."

"Yeah, I think that would be great. Like, 'water in the desert'—like an oasis!" Celeste looked up all of a sudden. "We could do all sorts of oasis stuff—like piles of sand and some palmetto trees in pots."

Nick leaned forward excitedly. "Yeah, and I know this great band we could get—they might come up here if I asked them—and they're called Mirage."

"That's perfect! And we could have those fluttery transparent banners we talked about before, and designer water," Celeste said, scribbling fast.

"Here you are," a loud voice said above them. Celeste looked up, startled, as the waitress slapped the check down on the table. She'd been so caught up in the party planning, she'd almost forgotten where they were.

Nick threw down a few bills and extracted himself from the booth, wiping his mouth with a crumpled napkin. He extended a hand to Celeste, who took it, surprised. His palm felt dry and rough, like a paw. She heaved herself out of the booth.

As they zoomed back to town at eighty miles an hour, Nick suddenly banged the steering wheel with one hand. "I've got it!" he said loudly over the wind.

"What?" Celeste yelled through the hair that was pasting itself to her face.

"We need to get inspired. Have you ever seen *Lawrence of Arabia*? The desert scenes are just the right kind of atmosphere we need for the party—you know, to go with the 'water in the desert' theme. Why don't we watch it tonight? To really understand our vision." Nick signaled and pulled in through the gate of Pinyon. The Alfa Romeo purred to a stop.

Celeste looked across at him warily. The breakfast had been really fun, and they'd treated each other almost like humans. So was he returning to the old Nick now that they were back at the resort? The silence must have stretched out a little too long, because Nick threw the car into park and looked out through the windshield.

"Hey," he said. "Totally business—I swear." He glanced over at her. "What, are you afraid of the big bad wolf, little girl?" he teased.

Celeste rolled her eyes. "Don't hold your breath. You're going to have to do better than that to scare me." She opened the door and then turned back to Nick. "I'm not off until nine. I'll be at your place at nine thirty, okay?"

"Yeah, see you then."

# Chapter Sixteen

✦

Celeste couldn't help feeling a little exposed that night as she rang the doorbell of the Saunders guesthouse. It was weird coming over in jeans and her favorite navy tank top instead of her uniform. She clutched her notebook in one hand and all of a sudden wondered if she should have brought some food or something. A few beers? Then she shook her head. Why was she acting like this was a date? This was about the party.

Nick opened the door. "Hey," he said.

"Hey," Celeste replied. They just stood there for a long minute, and then Nick hastily stepped back from the door.

"Sorry!" he said. "Come on in."

"Thanks." Celeste stepped over the threshold, glancing behind her. The last thing she needed was Travis popping out from behind a bush and making this into something it clearly wasn't. She followed Nick into the guesthouse. Most of the lights were off. "Where are your parents?" she asked, looking around. Nick shrugged.

"There was some big benefit tonight in the city. They took the Mercedes in. I think they'll be back by morning, but who knows?"

"Couldn't you go too?" Celeste asked, following Nick into the den. There were just a couple of lamps glowing dimly. A squishy gray couch piled with pillows faced a plasma TV on the wall.

"Are you kidding?" Nick snorted. "The last thing anyone wants is some teenage kid hanging around, eating all the hors d'oeuvres. I think my parents have taken me to one event my whole life, and that was when my own grandmother was giving it." He motioned to the couch. "I thought we could sit in here."

Celeste flopped down and almost disappeared into the gray cushions. "This is quite a couch. I didn't know we had this in here."

"Um, yeah." He dusted off a cushion and smiled sheepishly. "Do you want some of this weird European soda my mom's really into? It's passion fruit–flavored."

"That sounds good."

He was back in two minutes with a tray bearing two glasses and two funky little bottles, a giant bowl of popcorn, and a smaller bowl of M&M's. He set everything down on the ottoman and plopped down on the sofa.

Celeste grabbed a handful of popcorn and stared at the screen as the opening credits rolled. Nick wasn't sitting near enough to touch her, but she could feel him next to her anyway, as if her skin had grown a whole set of invisible antennae. She snuck a glance at him. He was stuffing handfuls of popcorn into his mouth and staring at the screen, where a bunch of men in robes were riding across the desert. He seemed totally oblivious to her presence. She stared for a minute at his forearms, which were tanned and covered with hair bleached from the sun, then forced herself to look back at the TV.

"You know that Peter O'Toole almost got trampled by horses during the filming?" he asked, his eyes not leaving the screen.

"Oh yeah?" Celeste replied, keeping her eyes fixed straight ahead. *Strictly business*, she reminded herself.

After about an hour, Nick paused the DVD and stretched. Celeste massaged her neck. "Alec Guinness is awesome in this," she said, stretching her arms over her head.

"Yeah. He's so good. Have you ever seen *Smiley's People*?"

Celeste shook her head. "When did that come out?"

"Well, it's not a movie, it was a TV series based on

John le Carré novels. Anyway, John le Carré said that after he saw Alec Guinness play Smiley, he couldn't even write the character anymore without thinking of Alec Guinness."

Normally, Celeste would've just assumed Nick was showing off. But he sounded so genuinely interested in what he was saying and in fact, he wasn't even looking at her. He was picking a bit of popcorn out of his teeth.

"That's really interesting," she said slowly. All those years of flirting and Nick's over-the-top snobitude, and here they were, having a real conversation—actually, their second in one day. Celeste almost looked around for hidden cameras, but it seemed like maybe she wasn't being punk'd after all. He smiled right at her and for a minute, their eyes connected. His face seemed to fill up her field of vision, and for a moment she flashed back to their final drunken kiss at the end of last summer. Both of them laughing, almost spilling their beers, and then his arms around her waist and his mouth on hers. He'd tasted like mint and alcohol.

Celeste's phone buzzed. She jumped and ripped her eyes away from Nick's, clapping her hand on her pocket at the same time. "Oh, my phone!" she exclaimed a little too loudly.

"Yeah. You'd better answer it," Nick replied. He stared at her for a second longer and then started stirring the leftover popcorn kernels in the bowl with his finger, looking oddly disappointed.

Celeste peeked at the screen and leaped to her feet, knocking her thighs into the coffee table when she saw Travis's name.

"Whoa." Nick reached out and steadied the soda bottles. "What's up?"

*Beep.* Travis had left a voice mail. Damn it. Now he was going to wonder where she was.

"Heh-heh." Celeste laughed nervously. "Um, can I use your bathroom?"

"Sure," Nick said. He clicked the TV on to *Sports-Center.* "But I hope it's not just to freshen up. I like my girls kinda dirty." He caught Celeste's startled glance and laughed. "Joking."

Celeste felt a little splash of irritation well up in her. Here she'd been thinking how nice it was when he treated her like a person instead of a potential hookup, and now he'd regressed straight back to annoying and snobby.

"Don't worry," she snapped, heading toward the bathroom. "You've never been worth the effort of freshening up."

In the peach and pale green bathroom, which was bigger than her entire bedroom at home, Celeste perched on the closed toilet seat and dialed Travis.

"I'm sitting here on the golf course. It's dark and

there's no one around," he said as soon as he answered. "And I've got two bottles of Stella. Where are you?"

Celeste glanced nervously at the door, thanking God for the millionth time that people couldn't see through phones. "Um, out with Devon," she said, trying to keep her voice low yet normal-sounding.

"Where are you guys? You didn't tell me you were going out," Travis said. "And why are you talking all muffled like that?"

"I'm not talking muffled." Celeste raised her voice a tiny bit. "It was a last-minute thing. Devon came by with . . . Paul Simon tickets, so we went. I didn't have time to call you." She stared at a small spider making its way across the peach bath mat.

"Wait, you're at a *Paul Simon* concert?" Travis asked incredulously. "Right now? Why's Paul Simon playing Palm Springs? And why's it so quiet?"

"He's—um, it's a small concert. A really small concert," Celeste stammered. "He's only playing one night . . . at his grandmother's house." *What, Celeste?* "It's like an invitation-only thing, so there aren't that many people here." The spider had reached the sink pedestal and begun its journey up to the basin.

"Wait, so let me get this straight," Travis said with irritating logic. Why couldn't she have talked to him later in the evening, *after* he'd drunk those Stellas? "You're at Paul Simon's grandmother's house in Palm Springs, listening to an invite-only concert. Is that right?"

"Right," Celeste said desperately, eyeing the door. She'd been in here way too long. Nick was going to think she had some serious intestinal issues. "Oh, whoops! They're starting again. Gotta go. I'll talk to you tomorrow, okay?" She clicked off.

Celeste opened the bathroom door and leaned against the door frame for a minute. She felt like she needed a nap. A medal and then a nap, actually. Slowly, she made her way back down the hall toward the den, where she could still hear the TV blasting. But as she passed an open bedroom door, Celeste stopped. There, on the desk, she spotted a MacBook Air, one of those really light new laptops. The room was obviously Nick's: T-shirts lay strewn over the chair and floor, and several pairs of sneakers were jumbled by the unmade bed. Celeste stared in envy at the shiny white computer on the desk.

"Like my new baby?" Nick said from behind her. Celeste jumped.

"Oh! Uh, yeah. I was just, um, lost," she said hastily, backing away from the door. She felt like she'd been caught reading his diary.

He didn't seem like he cared, though. He stepped into the room and patted the laptop tenderly. "I love this baby. I can do all my film editing on it practically."

"I've had my eye on one of those too," Celeste said,

trying to swallow the envy in her voice. *Of course he has exactly the laptop I'd want—he probably gets a new one every six months,* she thought.

He glanced over at her quickly. "I got it at a computer store I worked at one Christmas break. It was a floor model and the manager gave me an amazing deal. I do actually work for things I want."

Celeste felt her cheeks turn pink. "Um, okay. How about that movie?" she said, backing away from the door and heading back toward the den. Nick followed but stopped in the kitchen.

"I'm starved," he announced. "You want a sandwich?"

"Yeah, sure." She sat down in one of the kitchen chairs and watched as Nick bustled around like one of the hot Food Network chefs, pulling rolls out of a bag and slapping on huge piles of roast beef, cheddar cheese, lettuce, and tomato, all covered liberally with mustard. He handed a loaded plate to Celeste, who gazed at it in amazement. "What do you think I am, a linebacker?" She laughed.

"Oh yeah," he said through a mouthful of roll. "Don't worry, I'll finish yours."

Back in the den, he settled himself on the sofa, balancing the sandwich plate on his stomach. Celeste settled herself gingerly next to him. She took a bite of roast beef. Boy-made snacks, a movie—this felt like a date. She shook her head violently. No. It did not feel like a date, because she wasn't with Travis—her boyfriend—the boy she went on dates with.

"What do you have, a bug in your ear or something?" Nick asked, chewing with his cheeks distended.

"Oh! No, I'm fine," she said quickly. Nick started the movie again and she gazed blankly at the camels and horses trawling across the screen. She was going to have to be more discreet about her internal battles. Because it was starting to seem like she was the one who needed help keeping this relationship professional.

# Chapter Seventeen

✦

Well, I don't know why you have to go," Travis said. Or rather, whined. He peered out the windshield at the maze of warehouses and concrete buildings. "I have no idea where we are anyway."

Celeste sighed and tried to push down the irritation rising in her. "I told you. Nick and I really want this band for the party, but they won't come out to the resort for an audition. The only time they'd let us hear them is when they're warming up for their concert tonight." Inside, Celeste knew that she was actually stoked to see the band play. Although she'd really rather *not* be stuck in the car with a whiny boyfriend. But her parents' car was in the shop, and her dad had agreed that Travis could drive her in a resort truck only if he

147

stopped on the way back and picked up some new mower blades. She'd figured a one-way trip with a whiny Travis would be better than however long it would take her to explain why she was riding with Nick. She was starting to rethink that decision.

"And," Travis went on, swinging the truck down a narrow alley lined with fire escapes, "I really don't like the idea of you driving back with him."

Celeste fought the urge to roll her eyes. Instead, she peered down at the directions once more. "Is this Highland?" she asked, squinting up at the nonexistent street signs.

"How the hell should I know?" Travis growled, reversing to avoid a one-way street.

"Travis, chill out," Celeste said. "We're practically right on top of it—turn! Highland!"

Travis braked suddenly and screeched the truck to the right. He pulled up in front of a scarred metal door set into the side of a crumbling, graffitied building.

"I'll see you tomorrow, okay?" Celeste said, opening the door. "And don't worry—this is all totally business! Remember what I told you about keeping the Saunderses happy."

Travis nodded sullenly and drove off.

Celeste struggled with the latch on the battered metal door. Finally she managed to press it down, and the door flew open with a terrific crash against the interior wall. Celeste stumbled and almost fell into the room. To her embarrassment, the door opened directly onto the performance space. The band had been warming up on a stage across the room. The lead singer, whom Celeste recognized from their publicity shots, stopped in mid-wail and stared. Everyone else—a few sound guys, some rocker types sitting at little tables, and Nick—turned around to see who was making the grand entrance. Celeste smiled weakly into the silence and crept to a seat next to Nick. To complete her humiliation, the band didn't resume tuning up again until she was sitting down. Finally, the lead singer shook his greasy shoulder-length hair and played a few notes on his guitar. "Let's take that again, guys," he called.

Under the cover of the music, Celeste leaned over to whisper to Nick, "This place is freaky!" She looked around at the exposed pipes on the brick walls, the black-painted plywood stage, the grimy bar at the back of the room, where a tattooed bartender was setting up glasses in preparation for the night's concert. The floor was sticky under her flip-flops.

"Yeah, I know," Nick murmured back. "It's like a nineteen eighty-five time warp." He gazed at the band on stage. They were all skinny and deathly pale. "They look like they spend all their time underground, but they were band of the month in *Rolling Stone*. The singer is Sloan Love, by the way."

Sloan was doing some sort of bizarre howling vocal warm-up onstage. "He sounds like his volume control is broken," Celeste said. "I think the guests will all start running away if he sings like that, if the creeptastic eye makeup doesn't scare them off first."

Nick laughed, watching the stage. "I think that's just his warm-up. Let's hear how they sound once they do a song."

"First *Lawrence of Arabia*, now the next generation of Poison? What are you getting me into?" Celeste teased.

Nick widened his eyes. "Hey, I'm just trying to give us all the options." He sat back in his chair and draped his arm over the back of hers. Celeste eyed the arm for a minute and decided he really was just resting it there.

The band played for a few more minutes, and then ground to a sudden halt when Sloan made a chopping motion behind his back without looking back. They were all still for a moment and he raised his hand, still staring straight ahead. He brought it down onto his guitar and the band crashed into some opening chords.

At first, Celeste didn't hear the lyrics. She was completely caught up in the rich, complex melody flowing from the scruffy guys on stage. Given the tight, torn T-shirts and copious amounts of guyliner on stage, the band's hauntingly beautiful sound was entirely unexpected. Then Nick nudged her side. "They're singing to *you*!" he whispered.

"What?" Celeste said.

"*Celeste, like the stars in the sky, my Celestial,*" Sloan sang with his eyes closed.

"How do they even know my name?" Celeste tried not to shriek.

"I don't know—I mean, I sent an e-mail to say that we were coming, but no one ever wrote back. But if it's a coincidence, that's gotta be a sign that this is meant to be." Nick laughed.

Onstage, Sloan opened his eyes and stared right at Celeste as he finished the song. His black eyes were piercing. As the last wailing notes of the guitar died away, everyone was silent for a moment before breaking into scattered applause. The band put down their instruments and started wiping their foreheads and gulping from bottles of water. Sloan turned to confer with the drummer. Nick stood up and turned to look at her. "Okay, what do you think?"

Celeste nodded. "That was amazing," she said slowly.

"I thought so too," Nick agreed. "Should we book them?"

"Definitely."

"Okay. Let's go." He turned and headed toward the stage. Celeste trailed a little ways behind. She was surprised to find her palms sweating a little. She'd never really dealt with business contacts outside of Pinyon. And Sloan, as they approached, looked intimidatingly tall and aloof, with his prominent hipbones encased in worn black leather.

Nick, however, seemed unfazed. He hopped onto the edge of the stage like he talked to burgeoning rock stars all the time. The band took as much notice of them as if they'd been crumpled gum wrappers on the floor. Nick cleared his throat. Sloan put down his microphone and walked to the opposite side of the stage to adjust one of the dials on an amp. Celeste cast Nick a worried look, but his face was neutral.

"Hey," Nick said politely. No one even glanced at them. Celeste was starting to feel remarkably stupid just standing at the front of the stage. She felt like she had the day she'd tried ask Brian Hellman to be her boyfriend on the playground in fifth grade. He had proceeded to laugh at her and then tell all her friends.

"Nick," she murmured. "I don't think they're interested."

"Don't worry," he muttered back. Then he raised his voice. *"Hey!"* he almost shouted. His voice echoed in the empty space. Sloan turned around slowly. He stared at them for what felt to Celeste like a long, long moment. The other members of the band also stopped talking and turned to stare.

"Yeah?" Sloan said finally.

Nick offered a wide, toothy smile. "You guys sounded great."

Sloan looked bored. Nick plowed ahead, apparently unfazed. "We'd like to book you for our party at the Pinyon resort."

The singer waved his hand. "We don't do Sweet Sixteens, kid," he sniffed. "Thanks for coming, though." He turned back to the amp. Celeste felt like she'd been slapped in the face. She turned away.

"Where are you going?" Nick whispered, catching at her arm. She glared at him.

"I'm getting out of here—this guy is totally not interested in us. Let's just leave," she pleaded.

Nick's eyes narrowed and his dark blond eyebrows knit together. "No way," he said firmly, and, still hanging on to Celeste's arm, he clambered right up onto the dusty, scarred wooden stage. Celeste just managed to scramble up after him.

As the other band members watched in astonishment, Nick strode right to the other end of the stage and tapped Sloan on the shoulder. He turned around and, seeing who it was, rolled his eyes. Nick ignored this.

"I don't think you heard me just now," Nick said pleasantly. To Celeste's ears, he sounded as calm as someone ordering brunch at an outdoor café. "We're planning a party at the Pinyon Ranch for the Palm Springs Film Festival. This is going to be a big deal, so I'm not sure why you're not interested in gaining some exposure for your band." He gestured around the space. "What are you going to pull in tonight—a hundred people? Maybe one fifty?" Sloan's mouth was slightly open. Nick went on. "We're expecting over five hundred at the festival, and all of them will see your name on our promotional material. And we're talking entertainment insiders, not kids on summer vacation. But if you're not interested, no problem. We can easily find someone else."

Celeste's jaw dropped. That boy had balls! Who would have guessed that pretty boy Nick could face down Marilyn Manson Two? And he was being polite about it, even though the guy was obviously a total jerk. Sloan looked equally surprised but quickly regained his composure.

"We really don't have any interest in private parties," he sneered, his nostrils flaring.

"We'll double whatever fee you're getting for tonight's performance."

Celeste coughed. Nick was going to flatten their music budget—and probably the rest of the budget too. "Nick," she whispered, resisting the urge to tug at his sleeve. He ignored her.

The singer seemed to actually be considering Nick's offer. He dug a little black notebook out of his pocket and flipped through it, licking his forefinger each time he flipped one of the onionskin pages and muttering to himself. He fished out a stubby little pencil and poised it over one of the pages "All right," he said. "It'll be a waste of a night. When's your party?"

Celeste tried to restrain herself from jumping up and down right there on the scarred black stage, but Nick didn't even blink as he gave Sloan the details about where and when and promised to e-mail the info as well. Celeste thought she could detect just a hint of flush in his cheeks though.

They confirmed the band's contact information, then made their escape. As they shoved open the heavy metal door and stepped out onto the sidewalk in a flood of bright sunlight, Celeste threw her arms around Nick. "That was amazing!"

"Thanks," he said. Suddenly, Celeste realized what she was doing. She could feel the warmth of his skin beneath her arms, and their faces were only a few inches apart. She dropped her arms fast and backed away, tripping a little on a raised part of the sidewalk.

"Um, yeah," she said, pointlessly brushing her hair back from her face even though it was in a ponytail. "No, seriously, that was really good."

Nick shrugged. "Come on, the car's this way." He started heading down the sidewalk. "Honestly, it's not hard to get someone to listen to you. I hate that people always feel like they can blow off teenagers. I've learned that you just have to be polite, even if they're being rude. And you know he was totally bluffing about not being interested. He put your name in a song! That guy just enjoys being an ass."

"Yeah," Celeste said thoughtfully. Suddenly, she remembered what Nick had offered to pay them and felt herself deflate. "But, um, Nick, we'll never be able to afford them."

Nick didn't look concerned. "Yeah, we will. What, do you think I'd willingly break our budget? I'm not stupid, you know. I actually do know what a budget is." As they walked down the decaying block, he dug a piece of paper from his pocket. "One of my buddies keeps a website for music managers that lists what different venues pay. I took a look at it before we came over." He unfolded the paper and handed it to Celeste. "See? This place only pays one fifty. I mean, look at it. You're local and you've never been there before. We can totally afford three hundred for music."

Celeste glanced at the paper and looked carefully at Nick, who was ambling along the sidewalk. His white T-shirt clung to his wiry chest, and his straight blond hair was falling in his eyes as usual. It was nice having someone else take care of things once in a while, she thought. Instead of chasing Travis around, trying to pick up the pieces of his various screwups. *No, stop. Travis is awesome and fun*, she reminded herself hastily.

They reached the Alfa Romeo, parked halfway up on the curb and directly in front of a giant NO PARKING ANY TIME sign.

"Wow. I guess you're not quite as good at parking as you are at negotiating," Celeste teased.

"That sign was totally not there before," Nick insisted, his eyes wide.

Celeste slid into the front seat and Nick started the engine. "So, do you know how to get back to the resort from here?" she asked. "I have no idea."

"Totally," Nick reassured her. "I'll just go back the same way I came." The car thumped off the curb and he pulled into the street.

"Um, Nick?" Celeste said after a minute. "This is a one-way street. And you're going the wrong way."

"Damn!" Nick dragged the steering wheel over to one side and executed a perfect U-turn in the middle of the street. He turned onto another one-way street, this one deserted and lined with trash cans.

"Do you see a street sign?" he asked, peering up at the corner.

"Um, no. I think this is an alley. Why don't we try that way?" She pointed ahead, where they could see busy cars crossing a wide boulevard.

"Good idea." Nick floored the accelerator and the car shot ahead.

"By the way," Celeste said, "I'm glad you know where you're going, because I am totally turned around. Plus, all the signs are in Spanish now."

"Crap," Nick said, looking behind him and trying to switch lanes. "I have a confession. I have no idea where we are. Or how to use the GPS thing." He peered at the endless streets around them, with colorful signs in Spanish and bodegas and cell-phone shops lining the sidewalks. Suddenly, Celeste pointed ahead.

"Hey," she said. "Is that a park?" At the end of the street, they could see an expanse of grass and, just beyond it, a glimmer of blue water.

"It definitely is. And it looks like there's a little lake or something." Nick glanced over at Celeste. "How about a break?"

Celeste resisted the urge to look at her watch. She was technically due back at the resort *right* after the band audition, according to her father, but the water ahead looked so tempting. And didn't she deserve a little break during her summer of hard slogging? She glanced over at Nick. "Sure," she said. "Let's do it." Every one of her brain cells knew this was a bad idea. But none of them stopped her from jumping out of the car.

# Chapter Eighteen

◆

They'd pulled up on a little strip of asphalt near the park. The noise and traffic of the city blared behind them, but if Celeste faced forward, all she could see was smooth green grass and gravel paths. The lake Nick had pointed out lapped at the grassy bank about fifty feet way. A sign near them read RATHBONE MEMORIAL PARK. The place was almost totally deserted. Just a few figures were scattered across the green, strolling with dogs, or sitting on blankets. Celeste inhaled as the breeze lifted her ponytail.

The car door slammed next to her, and suddenly Nick grabbed her hand. "Come on!" he said, and raced her toward the lake.

Celeste paused at the edge of the small lake. The

gray-blue water glimmered in the sun. Peering forward, she could just make out a sandy bottom under the ripples. She kicked off her flip-flops and waded in, letting the cool water splash around her ankles. Behind her, Nick was laboriously unlacing his sneakers. "Come on!" she shouted. "This is why you have to wear flip-flops!"

"Just wait until I get over there," Nick shouted back. "You'll be sorry you ever met me."

"I already am!" Celeste called. Turning, she waded a little deeper, holding the skirt of her sundress up around her thighs, careful not flash Nick. Suddenly, a pair of strong arms grabbed her around the waist from behind and Nick lifted her high into the air. Celeste screamed and Nick flung her over one shoulder and started striding deeper into the water. "I'm going to kill you!" Celeste yelled, beating on his back with her fists. She thought of her white sundress and (gulp) white underwear—*and* no bra—and said a brief, fervent prayer that he wouldn't drop her in the water. Luckily, Nick spun her around a few times and then set her on her feet in the knee-deep water.

"Oh, you're going to get it now," Celeste said, advancing slowly toward him. She kicked at the water.

"Hey!" he protested, looking down at his wet shirt. "How can you expect me to not get you back for that?"

Celeste laughed and turned, running away as best she could in the water, lifting both her skirt and her knees high. Nick splashed after her, and she tried to run faster. She felt his fingers graze her back and then suddenly, there was an even bigger splash and she felt a wave of water hit her back. She looked behind her but there was no Nick.

"Nick?" she called, looking around. Nothing. "Nick?" she called again. Still nothing. Suddenly, with a heave, he emerged from the water, dripping and totally soaked. His shorts hung off him, running with water, and his shirt was transparent.

Celeste choked a little and bit the inside of her cheek to keep from laughing. He looked so forlorn, standing there with his hair plastered to his head. A few chortles escaped her and finally, she gave in, laughing so hard she had to double over and hold her stomach for a minute.

Nick just stood there while she laughed, his hands hanging at his sides and a woebegone expression on his face. When her giggles finally petered out, he looked at her through the wet strands of hair over his eyes. "Don't you know it's not nice to laugh at those less fortunate than you?"

Celeste swallowed another set of giggles and held out her hand. "I'm sorry—you just look really funny." Privately, she was thankful that it was Nick who was standing there soaked in water and not her. At least his pants weren't see-through.

Nick took her hand and together, they sloshed

through the water back to the bank. Nick dropped to the grass. "Let's hang out for a minute and I'll let my clothes dry." He stripped off his shirt and wrung it out, spreading it in the sun next to him.

"Um . . ." Celeste looked at her watch, trying not to stare at his lean chest and ropy, corded arms. "I should probably be getting back."

Nick patted the ground next to him. "Ten minutes. I can't get back into the Alfa Romeo this wet—if I drip on that leather, my dad will disown me." He tried to squeeze some water out of his shorts.

Celeste sank down and carefully stretched her wet legs out in front of her. The grass prickled against the backs of her calves. She lay back and stared at the endless blue sky vaulting overhead. It *did* feel good to just veg out here, with only the sound of the breeze in her ears, and no one asking her for a clean towel or a glass of water with only limes and no lemons. Nick lay down next to her and tucked his hands under his head. For a long moment, they were just quiet.

Then Nick asked, "So, what's the story with you two anyway?" Celeste's eyes sprang open. She raised her head.

"What?"

"What's the deal with you two?"

"Who?"

"You and Travis."

She lowered her head warily and affected noncha-lance. "What do you mean, what's the deal? He's my boyfriend." She could hear a little tension entering her voice. *A couple of days of getting along and now he's going to bring up Travis. Great.*

Nick's eyes were shut tight against the sun and his face was expressionless. "I just wouldn't put the two of you together, you know, if you asked me." His voice was soft and calm, but something about it irritated Celeste. She sat up.

"What are you talking about? Travis is a really nice guy, for your information. We've been together almost a year now." Her voice rose at the end.

"Okay, that's cool." Nick still didn't move or open his eyes. "I'm just kind of surprised you're into him. He doesn't seem that bright."

"What?" Now Celeste's voice rose into a screech. "Who are you to be talking about bright? As far as I can tell, all you ever do is lie around, flirt with girls, and play with your daddy's money."

Nick flinched as if she'd hit him. He didn't say any-thing. Celeste got to her feet and dusted off the rear of her dress. The sun felt like it was baking her face, and the wind had picked up. It whistled hotly past her face like the air in an oven.

"I want to go back," Celeste said tightly.

"Fine." He got up, not looking at her.

The asphalt burned under her feet as Celeste tramped back across the grass to the car. She stood by the locked door of the car, waiting for Nick and fuming. How dare he insult Travis like that? Here she'd been thinking that they were working really well together planning the party, and then the minute she'd let her guard down, he'd swooped right in and started trying to make trouble between her and Travis again.

The car beeped and she looked across the parking lot. Nick had unlocked it with his remote. She slid into the baking interior and sat there with the door open. Nick climbed in and started the engine. Silently, he tossed two wet objects into her lap. Celeste looked down at them, confused, before she recognized her discarded flip-flops.

"I had my personal valet pick these up for you," Nick said, looking behind him to back out of the parking lot. "It's what all of us lazy rich boys do."

Silently, Celeste slipped them onto her feet. She folded her hands in her lap and gazed out the window at the highway slipping by.

The silence lay thickly over the car. They passed a sign for Highway 95 and Nick turned onto it. In twenty minutes, they were pulling through the main gates of the guesthouse. Neither of them had spoken a single word since leaving the park. Nick pulled up in front of the main building and Celeste put her hand on the door handle, ready to jump out as soon as he stopped the car.

He braked and she swung open the door. "Wait," he said suddenly, putting his hand on her bare knee. Celeste hesitated. She just wanted to get out of there, but Nick's face looked so plaintive that she reluctantly swung her leg back into the car and faced him again.

"What?" she said.

He took his hand off her knee. "Look," he said. "I'm sorry—I was an idiot back there. I just talk out of my ass sometimes."

"Yeah, I'll say," Celeste snapped. But Nick didn't flare up. He just stared at his lap until Celeste felt a little bad for her ungracious response.

"Whatever's going on with you and Travis is none of my business, okay? I'll just keep my rich-boy self away from him."

Celeste winced. "I'm sorry about that. It just came out. But I don't want you stirring up trouble with me and Travis." She paused. He looked over at her, almost pinning her against the car door with his hot blue gaze. Suddenly, the air in the car felt unbearably close. Celeste fumbled for the door handle. "I have to get out of here, okay?"

Nick nodded without looking at her. She could see the muscles of his clenched jaw standing out under his skin. He gripped the steering wheel and stared. "So, planning meeting tomorrow night?" he asked.

Celeste nodded and swung her legs back out of the

car. "Yeah. See you in the dining room at nine." She shut the door and stood watching as the Alfa Romeo purred away toward the Saunders guesthouse. Celeste stood in the middle of the path, her hands hanging forlornly by her sides. Earlier, she'd thought she'd been too hard on Nick, but once again, he'd proved himself the arrogant jerk he'd always been. She started walking slowly back to the bungalow. But if Nick really was just trying to stir her up, why was she letting him get to her? She and Travis belonged together, so Nick's opinion shouldn't even faze her. Unfortunately, telling herself that didn't make her any less fazed.

# Chapter Nineteen

✦

G od, it's hot," Celeste said, on her hands and knees in the soft dirt. She troweled up another hole and carefully set the flower plant in it. The sun was beating down on her back, right through her white polo shirt. She'd managed to find a way to work with Travis for a day, to make up for spending so much time with Nick–not that Travis knew that was the reason. Unfortunately, that meant planting petunias in the blazing heat all morning by the new guesthouses that were being built on the other side of the golf course.

"Yeah," Travis agreed. He lifted another flat of the flowers out of the wheelbarrow. "I'm almost out of water too."

"We'll have to get some more from the main

building," Celeste said. She sat up on her heels and wiped at her forehead with her arm, the only part of her that wasn't dusty. There wasn't anyone around—the guesthouses wouldn't be ready for another couple of weeks and the workmen were apparently taking the day off.

Suddenly, Travis lay down his trowel. "Hey, I've got an idea," he said.

"What?" Celeste asked. Any idea would be better than this medieval labor. Why, why had she volunteered to do this, instead of her usual work, which would have been paperwork in the office? Boring, but at least it would have been cool.

"We've been planting for, like, two hours," Travis said. "Let's go cool off in one of the guesthouses. The guys put air-conditioning in the other day. We need a break."

Celeste blinked. "Um, well, we're not really supposed to be in the empty guesthouses." Dad didn't want any-one dirtying up the carpet or anything before guests even stayed there.

Travis leaned closer. "Come on! It'll be nice and cool in there and . . . I promise a back massage to any girl who takes a break with me." He rubbed her shoulders.

Celeste considered. The main building was a fifteen-minute walk away across the golf course, and no one would know they were taking a break in a guesthouse if they were careful. She lay down her own trowel and cracked her back, gazing at her dirt-dusted, sweaty arms. "Okay, but I'm just warning you—if we get caught, I'm going to swear you dragged me in there kicking and screaming." She tried to channel Nick's devilish grin.

Travis grabbed her hand. "Come on." They got to their feet and made their way to one of the buildings. Celeste glanced around and then slid her card into the door slot and pushed it open. The place was hot and stuffy and smelled like new paint. The airy rooms were still unfurnished, but the carpet was laid in the main living room.

"Let's get the AC on," Travis said, striding over to the thermostat. Almost immediately, a stream of icy air began flowing out of the vent near Celeste, curling deliciously around her ankles.

"Oh my God, that feels amazing." She went over to the sink in the empty kitchen and started running cold water over her arms and face. She splashed some on the back of her neck and wished she could just take a shower. She looked at Travis, who was randomly opening the cabinet doors. They'd never get back to the main building at this rate. Travis turned his back to check the thermostat again, and Celeste cupped her hands, filling them with water. She took aim and flung the icy water at Travis, hitting him square on the back of the neck.

"Hey!" he shouted. "Oh, you are in trouble." He

grabbed her around the waist and lifted her feet off the ground. Celeste giggled and he set her back on her feet.

"What's so funny?" he asked, slowly kissing the back of her neck. The sensation of his hot lips on her skin made Celeste shiver.

"Nothing," she said, turning toward him. Her voice echoed against the flat, empty walls. She wrapped her arms around his neck and he kissed her as she ran her hands up and down his back. Suddenly, he stooped and swung her up into his arms. Celeste squealed and Travis carried her over to the vast living room. She closed her eyes as he put her down on the thick carpet and then lay down next to her, pressing himself up against her.

A little while later, Celeste took a deep breath. Travis, now minus his shirt, dropped back on the carpet and wriggled his shoulder blades against the scratchy rug. "So, the boys are talking about going out tonight. You want to go? We haven't been out together in forever."

"Sure," Celeste said automatically. Then she stopped.

"What?" Travis asked.

"Nothing—it's just that I forgot I have a planning meeting with, um, Nick, tonight." She tried to swallow the word *Nick* in hopes that Travis would somehow miss it. No such luck.

He sat up on the rug, a flush darkening his cheeks. "Are you kidding? You spend all your time with him these days," he said, his voice rising. "Now he gets nights too?"

Celeste sat up too. *That's what I get for mentioning Nick.* "Look, I've told you a million times—it's my job. What do you want me to do?"

Travis pouted. "I've been really patient the last few weeks—"

"You have!" Celeste reassured him.

"But I'm getting sick of this. Do you actually *like* hanging out with this guy or what?"

"No! I mean, I don't mind him when he's not being a jerk, but I'm just trying to make this an amazing party. I mean, maybe if I prove I can do this, Dad'll let me off the hook next summer. Besides"—she put her hand on Travis's—"I really want to drive up to Tempe with you next month, and he'll totally let me once he sees how great everything is."

"Yeah," Travis agreed reluctantly.

"I mean, maybe they'd even let me spend fall break with you!"

To her surprise, Travis didn't look quite as excited at this thought as she'd thought he would. He got to his feet. "Um, yeah, that would be great," he said. He offered Celeste his hand and pulled her to her feet.

"Look, if you're that worried, why don't you just come with me to the meeting tonight? You can see all the stuff we're planning."

"Fine," Travis said, reaching for his polo shirt. "We should get back to work."

# Chapter Twenty

✦

"N ick!" Celeste called later that evening, poking her head into the silent dining room. All the tables were made up for breakfast the next morning—all except for one, where Nick sat, surrounded by papers and folders. There were several glasses and some plates sitting in a stack in front of him, and he was scribbling furiously on a legal pad. He looked up and grinned, but Celeste could see the grin fade as he spied Travis coming in behind her.

"Travis wanted to come and see how the plans are going," Celeste said, pulling out a chair. "That's cool, right?"

Nick shrugged. "Whatever," he said briefly, looking right through Travis as if he weren't even there. He shoved the legal pad toward Celeste. "I just finished making up a master list of all the stuff we still need to do."

Travis sat down and ostentatiously put an arm around Celeste's shoulders. He pulled her into him and started rubbing the side of her neck. Celeste glanced at Nick. He was watching the display with his lip slightly curled. Oh, this was not going to be the most relaxing night of her life. She resisted the urge to shrug off Travis's massaging fingers and pulled Nick's legal pad toward her instead. She scanned the list. "Vendors, tastings—" She pulled away from Travis slightly. "Um, thanks, Travis, I'm good now." He stared at her resentfully for a second and then dropped his arm, rocking back in his chair and aiming a challenging glare at Nick, who narrowed his eyes and glared back.

"Don't worry, babe, I'll give you a better massage later," Travis said to Celeste, although he was still staring straight at Nick.

Nick shuffled a few papers around. His face was cool and bland. "I'm impressed you know a big word like *massage*, Travis. I guess all that mowing out in the sun hasn't fried too many brain cells after all," he said smoothly.

Travis's fist clenched convulsively on the tablecloth and Celeste grabbed his arm to head off the impending train wreck.

"Wow, you're so organized," she said to Nick, still hanging on to Travis's arm. She felt the muscles relax under her hand and gingerly let go, ready to grab it again if Travis pounced. "Who would have guessed?" To her relief, Nick grinned.

"I'm full of surprises," he said, aiming his comment directly at Travis. Travis frowned and dug his phone out of his pocket. Celeste glanced over as he started checking his messages.

She squashed down a little thread of irritation and examined the list again. "Okay, you want to do the table settings?" she asked Nick. He was staring at Travis and seemed on the verge of speaking but closed his mouth with a snap.

"Yeah. Here, I got some samples from the stock-room." He unstacked the different plates in front of him and started matching them up with glasses.

"Hmm." Celeste considered the five different arrange-ments in front of them. "What do you think, Travis?" she asked. She glanced over when he didn't answer. He was rapidly typing on his phone. "Who are you texting?" she asked, squashing the worm of irritation again.

He looked up. "What? Oh, the guys are getting ready to go out."

Celeste blew air out of her nose and glanced at Nick. He arched one eyebrow. "Where are you all meeting?" she asked.

"At those hot springs where we went to that party. I told the guys it's the best."

"Travis!" Celeste exclaimed in surprise. "You can't take the guys there. That's only supposed to be for Pinyon staff."

"It's the desert, Celeste. It's public," Travis said. Celeste noticed Nick watching the exchange with lively interest. She turned back to Travis.

"Whatever," she said. "Do whatever you want. I just think that spot would be better if everyone didn't know about it."

Travis exhaled. "Stop worrying, okay?" He shoved back his chair. "See you later, babe. Have fun with the plates." He leaned down and kissed Celeste on the mouth, complete with tongue. She tried to pull away after a moment but he held on to her. Why did she feel like a preschool teacher with a class of two?

There was a moment's silence after Travis left. "That went well," Nick offered.

Celeste rolled her eyes. "It did not."

Nick gave her his slick little smile. "I know. I was just trying to make you feel better."

Celeste punched him in the arm. "All right, let's get some work done." She started shuffling around the place settings. "Hey, by the way, when do you want to screen the film? We should block out, like, two hours, right?"

Nick looked embarrassed for a minute. He fidgeted

with a napkin. "Well, it's, um, only twenty minutes." He stared down at the table and then glanced up quickly, as if expecting Celeste to laugh or something.

"What? What's wrong with that?" she asked him.

"Well, most people are used to feature-length movies. So they usually smirk when they hear my film is only twenty minutes."

"Well, that's just stupid," Celeste told him firmly. "They just don't understand that there are other kinds of movies other than the big, splashy Hollywood type."

"Right!" Nick's face lit up. "I mean, it's like everyone expects a sex-in-the-shower scene and a car chase, or it's not a good movie."

Celeste tilted back in her chair, balancing on the two back legs. "So what's your film about? We've been planning this whole party and everything, and I keep forgetting that it's not just a party—it's actually all about the film."

Nick's tanned face started turning pink again, and Celeste thought in spite of herself that he looked cute when he blushed. It was also kind of cute that the arrogant Nick got embarrassed talking about his film.

"Well, actually, I um, brought it with me."

Celeste banged her chair forward on the floor. "You did?"

Nick's face was now so pink, he looked like he had a terrible sunburn. "Yeah. It's on my laptop." He lifted the

MacBook Air onto the table and then put his hands in his lap.

Celeste waited. "Well, okay, let's see it!" she finally said.

"Only if you're sure you really want to." Nick fumbled with the catch on the laptop lid.

Celeste scooted her chair around next to his and he opened a file labeled "Director's Cut." An intense wash of color immediately grabbed Celeste's attention. She watched, rapt, as an ocean crashed and, in the foreground, two sailboats raced side by side. A girl was sailing one and a guy was sailing another. The film had clearly been shot by someone who loved the ocean—Celeste really felt like she was part of the race. The sailors struggled to overtake each other until the girl finally won. The scene shifted and the girl and guy were shown tying up their boats in a harbor. They were staring at each other. Then an older man appeared and the girl went off with him, her head on his shoulder and her arm around his waist. For reasons she didn't entirely understand, Celeste felt an intense pang of sadness as the camera showed the guy on the dock, staring after them. The scene shifted again and the camera showed the outside of a small white house in a gorgeous, sun-drenched seaside town. The guy from the race walked up to the door and went inside. The girl from the harbor was waiting for him on the sofa. The camera faded to black.

Nick clicked the screen closed and wiped his hands on the sides of his jeans, as if his palms were sweaty. "So, what do you think?" he asked, looking at the table instead of Celeste.

She considered a moment.

"Okay, just say if you don't like it!" Nick burst out, his cheeks still pink.

"Hey, calm down," Celeste said. "I was thinking, that's all. I think it's really interesting—who was the girl? Why did she go off with the older guy?"

Nick looked up. "So you don't think it's totally amateurish?"

"No!" Celeste reassured him. "I mean, I don't know anything about film, but every shot was really beautiful. And the story builds quietly, you know? Like, you go through this range of emotions without even really knowing why."

Nick let out a giant sigh and flopped back in his chair. He dangled his arms and let his head fall back. "I was a little nervous showing it to you."

Celeste stifled her giggle. "Oh yeah? I could never tell. So come on, who was the girl?"

"Well, *I* know who she is," Nick said, straightening up and regaining some of his usual composure, "but I like to let the audience figure it out for themselves—I mean, she could be anybody. People can make her whoever they want."

Celeste sat back and draped her arm over the back of the chair. "Wow," she said. "That's good. I . . ." She looked down at her hands and let her sentence trail off.

"What?" Nick asked. "Wait, no, don't say—let me guess." He tapped a pencil on one of his teeth, pretending to think. "You're really surprised that a suave ladies' man like me could actually make something so delicate, insightful, sensitive, and thought-provoking. A movie so heartbreaking that it rivals even—"

"Stop!" Celeste held up her hands, laughing. "I'm just surprised. It's not what I expected from . . ." She stopped again.

"Spit it out," Nick said. He folded his hands as if waiting for a scolding.

Celeste smiled a little. "Well, from the annoying, spoiled kid who won't stop trying to flirt with me."

"I have to admit, something about you does bring out the flirt in me a little." Nick smiled.

"A little?" Celeste teased.

"Okay, a lot. You just look so cute when you get annoyed." He looked at the ceiling.

"Thanks a lot," she said. "Hey, are you hungry? It's almost midnight."

"Starving," Nick admitted. "You know my dormant inner asshole needs to be fed on a regular basis."

Celeste stood up. "Kitchen raid?"

"Wow," Nick said, following her through the big

swinging doors into the vast, immaculate, silent kitchen. "I feel like I'm entering some sort of inner sanctum."

"You are—the kitchen's like the Holy Grail of Pinyon." Celeste pried open one of the huge industrial refrigerators and gazed inside. "Usually, Solomon keeps stuff in here in case a guest demands, like, filet mignon at three a.m. or something." She rummaged among the metal tubs and plastic-wrapped dishes, her head and torso almost disappearing into the frosty interior of the fridge, and emerged with a big plate and a bowl. "Jackpot." She set the dishes on the counter. "Leftover chocolate soufflé and whipped cream." She grabbed two bowls from a nearby shelf.

"Oh my God, that looks incredible," Nick said. Using his fingers, he stuffed a bite into his mouth. "It *is* incredible. Taste this." He held out a glob of chocolate soufflé.

Celeste paused. *Don't be so uptight*, she told herself. She leaned forward and licked the soufflé off Nick's finger, letting the creamy, fluffy chocolate spread over her tongue. She closed her eyes for a minute, just savoring the taste, and then, opening them, realized that Nick's blue eyes were staring right into hers. She could feel his breath on her cheek. She stared back at him, their faces only a few inches apart. Then Celeste turned away so fast, she almost knocked her bowl of soufflé into the counter. "Well, we should probably get back to work," she said awkwardly, blundering through the doors and back into the dining room.

The next few hours flew by as Celeste and Nick bent over their papers and calendars spread out everywhere, making to-do lists and master lists, and hammering out schedules. By three o'clock, Celeste felt like her eyeballs had been coated in sand and dipped in salt water. She groaned and put down her pencil. When she closed her eyes, yellow sheets of lined paper and calendar pages danced in front of her eyes. "Oh my God, I definitely need a break." She twisted her back right and left, listening to the series of cracks. Beside her, Nick rubbed his red eyes and fell out of his chair, landing on the carpet with a crash.

"Are you okay?" Celeste asked, peering down at him.

"Fine," he mumbled, his face mashed into the rug. "Just wake me up when people start coming in for breakfast, okay?"

Celeste got up from her chair and reached down, hauling at his arm. "Get up. We're done anyway."

Nick hauled himself up from the carpet and they headed out into the dry, cool desert night. Celeste inhaled deeply. The fresh air smelled great after spending hours indoors. She and Nick walked down the red sandstone path side by side, their footsteps echoing against the silent buildings. Celeste wondered what had happened to the easy camaraderie of the meeting. She could sense the warmth of Nick beside her and accidentally bumped his shoulder as they walked. "Sorry!" they both said at the same time. There was a pause, and they looked at each other and laughed awkwardly. Celeste could feel the spot where he'd bumped her searing on her shoulder like a burn.

At the turnoff to the staff quarters, Celeste stopped and turned to face Nick. They looked at each other. The moonlight reflected off Nick's cheekbones, turning his eyes into deep hollows.

"Your skin looks silver," he said softly. For a long moment, Celeste stood frozen, and then she took a little step back.

"Um, see you tomorrow?" she almost whispered, wondering why her heart was pounding.

"Yeah," Nick said huskily. He turned and disappeared down the path.

Safe inside her room, with the warm yellow light dispelling all that dark tension outside, Celeste threw herself onto her bed. She curled up in a little ball and hugged her pillow to her chest. Where did all that come from? Celeste thought of kissing Nick at the party last year. That had been nothing—just drunk sloppiness. The party had been going on for a few hours, and everyone, including herself, had been pretty trashed. Madonna had been playing, and he'd leaned over and kissed her with a mouth that tasted like vodka. She hadn't really thought about it too much at the time, and she certainly hadn't felt anything. She hadn't really seen that kiss coming. But tonight, under the stars, she'd been able to see in his eyes how much he wanted to kiss her.

Celeste hugged her pillow tighter and squeezed her eyes shut. She fought off the rising feeling that, if she were perfectly honest with herself, she'd wanted to kiss him back.

# Chapter Twenty-one

◆

Celeste felt like her head was spinning around in circles as the festival drew closer. Every day, she and Nick—who thankfully seemed to have forgotten about the moment in the moonlight—ran around the resort like crazy people, making sure everything was in place. Aside from one of the waiters dropping an entire tray of glassware, everything was coming together.

A couple of days before the guests were set to arrive, Celeste was supervising the raising of the tent over the pool area. A group of sweaty, red-faced workmen were wrestling with the heavy white canvas, which kept snapping away from them in the high desert wind. Celeste could see that it was going to look fantastic when it was up—it covered the teak deck around one half of the pool, and the inside was going to be strung with shimmery blue and green lights.

One of the workmen was about to stick a stake right into one of the flower beds. "Hey!" Celeste yelled. "I mean, excuse me! Could you move that over a few feet? The flowers are right there." The guy looked up and nodded. Celeste sank her head back against the lounge chair. All she wanted to do was lie here in this chair for about another two days. But the workmen were now trying to shove the tent stakes into the tubs of palms placed around the deck. Celeste heaved a sigh and got up. She struggled to pull a tent stake out of a tub. Just as she yanked it from the sandy soil, her phone rang. She dug it out of her pocket and glanced at the screen. It was Devon.

"Hey, girl!" Celeste squealed, tucking the phone between her cheek and shoulder and wiping her dirty hands on the back of her shorts. "I haven't talked to you in forever!"

"I know." Devon's voice sounded tinny. "They keep us crazy busy here—we're in classes all day and then rehearsals at night. I'm meeting so many awesome people though—like actors from the Royal Shakespeare Company! Can you believe it?"

"That's so great," Celeste said. "How's Scotland? Is it amazing? Does it look like *Braveheart*?"

"Totally. I keep expecting Mel Gibson to show up in

all that blue face paint. Hey, how's everything going there? Are you excited for the festival?"

"Yeah," Celeste said. "I'm nervous though! There are going to be so many celebrity types around, and everything has to be perfect."

"Look, you're an awesome party planner," Devon reassured her. "I'm sure you've been working your ass off."

Celeste smiled at the phone and sat down on one of the pool lounges. "Yeah. Nick and I have been up until, like, dawn every night going over things."

"Oooh, how's *that* going?" Devon's voice dropped. "Have he and Travis torn each other's arms off yet or what?"

"No, they've been really good. I mean, I explained to Travis that it's just business and he was totally cool about it. I mean, he knows how important all this is."

"Yeah . . ." Devon sounded doubtful. "Travis has such a wicked temper though. Just watch it."

Celeste scowled a little. "Well, don't worry, he's not even going to be here. He's going to the beach that weekend with his buddies."

Loud whiny music started up on Devon's end of the phone. "What is that?" Celeste asked.

"Oh my God, it's bagpipes. Don't ask—they actually call us to our classes and meals that way. It's insane. I feel like I'm turning plaid. Anyway, I have to go to

monologue rehearsal. But I'll be home right after the festival, so at least you have that to look forward to!"

Celeste heard her named being called and looked up
to see her father standing in the doorway of the office,
his arms folded and his face already red—hopefully with
heat and not annoyance.

"Oh boy, got to go," Celeste said. "Dad alert. Be
good!"

"Not likely! Talk to you later." Devon clicked off.

Celeste shoved the phone into her pocket and walked
over to stand beside her father. She folded her arms too,
and for a long moment, they surveyed the hive of activ-
ity buzzing in front of them: the massive tent flapping,
workmen nailing up supports for the arches of palm
fronds, the huge bar being wheeled in, and the giant
tubs of flowers and ferns being unloaded from trucks
and placed around the perimeter of the pool deck.

Dad cleared his throat and Celeste looked up at him,
suddenly anxious. Did he think it was tacky or something? Maybe he was worried about money. She didn't
want him to regret giving her this responsibility. Celeste
fished around in her stack of papers for the budget and
cleared her throat.

"Dad, I know this all looks really crazy right now, but
believe me, it's going to come together great. And it's
actually under budget, if you can believe that." She
offered him the clipboard, which he accepted and

studied, leafing through the rest of her preparation papers: copies of invoices, lists, contact names, and cell numbers. "Look, Dad, we even have a spreadsheet with background on all the important guests—food preferences and allergies, special requests, and names of partners. One of the VIPs' wives is allergic to pepper, so we've even confirmed that the caterers will leave it out of the passed hors d'oeuvres completely." Celeste told him.

Her father raised his eyebrows and nodded slowly. He still hadn't spoken, and Celeste couldn't read his expression. He handed her back her clipboard and then squeezed her shoulder.

"Celeste," he rumbled. "You've always worked hard. I'm really proud of you. You've done a great job."

Celeste could feel her face turning pink. Her dad draped his heavy arm around her shoulders and gave her a brief hug before turning and heading back into the office. Celeste heaved a sigh of relief. The festival hadn't even started and she already felt like a success.

# Chapter Twenty-two

✦

Celeste stepped out of the shower and wrapped a towel around her head. The desert twilight was spreading its rays throughout her room, and the soft warm air was blowing through the window, but she didn't have to even glance outside. She could hardly believe it was actually here—the opening of the Palm Springs Film Festival. It seemed like with all the planning and anxiety and last-minute emergencies, the day itself would never come. But it was finally here. In half an hour, she had to be out at the main entrance to welcome the first set of guests. Then the opening cocktail party would start. And then Nick's party, the first big one of the festival, would be later that night.

Celeste smoothed on some Bath & Body Works

vanilla lotion. Laid out on her bed was definitely the coolest party dress she'd ever owned: a pink silk Marc Jacobs, knee-length, with a thick fold of fabric over one shoulder. And the shoes were Prada. She'd hardly been able to believe it when she'd found them at the Junk 'n' Jive vintage clothing store in town. She slipped the cool silk over her head and looked in the mirror. The dress fit perfectly, just skimming the curves of her body.

She applied a little mascara and lip stain with gloss on top and smudged a little smoky eyeliner on her upper lids. In this heat, anything else would slide right off her face. Her phone rang. Celeste snatched it off the dresser, her heart pounding.

"What is it?" Celeste answered.

"Hey, baby," Nick said on the other end. "You doing anything tonight? Want to hang out?"

Celeste tucked the phone under her cheek and dabbed on another layer of Benetint lip stain. "Very funny. Are you calling just to annoy me or is there actually a problem?"

"Maybe just a tiny one—the projection screen won't unroll. I think it's jammed." He sounded vaguely amused.

Celeste breathed a sigh of relief. Major crises she could not handle right now—minor crises, sure. "It was doing that earlier. You have to unroll it manually. Just get behind it. There's a crank near the top. Just crank it open and we'll leave it down for the party."

"Excellent. At least one of us has a brain around here." Celeste could hear the cracking of a back being stretched. "By the way, I don't think I'm going to come to the cocktail party. I better stay around here and make sure no one knocks the palm arches into the pool or anything."

Celeste shoved a little piece of paper with notes on key guests into her bag. "Is everything ready? Food, decorations, everything?"

"Yeah, it all looks great. Totally under control. Actually, the food's here now, so I better go tell that guy where to put it. He's trying to set everything on the drinks table." Nick chuckled.

"Go, go!" Celeste cried. "Quick!"

"Shhh, calm down. I'm going—see you later." He clicked off.

Celeste resisted the urge to start tearing at her cuticles and slipped her phone into her evening bag. If she came out of this evening without gray hair, it would be a miracle. She glanced at the clock and felt her heart rate spike. It was time to go out to the gates.

✦ ✦ ✦

Celeste stood near her parents and the Saunderses in the lobby, trying to not to fidget with her dress. The lobby was filled with well-dressed Hollywood types—everyone slim, lovely, and dressed with the perfect indie-film edge. Celeste tried not to gape at a woman wearing a torn black T-shirt and a huge diamond necklace talking to the guy in platform heels next to her. She glanced at her parents. They were beaming as they made pleasant small talk with the guests and accepted compliments on the resort. Celeste had never seen them happier.

Then she turned to peer through the main doors and her stomach plunged. There, getting out of a huge Escalade, were Travis and all five of his best buddies. They were talking and laughing as they slammed the car doors, taking off their sunglasses and surveying the place as if they already owned it. Celeste could feel her pulse pounding in her temples. What the *hell* were they doing here? She barreled through the glass doors and marched up to Travis.

"Hey, babe!" he greeted her. She could tell he'd already been drinking by the flushed, jovial look on his face, but luckily he didn't seem totally trashed—yet. Celeste forced a smile.

"Hi. Hi, guys." Everyone nodded.

"Hey, which way's the pool, Celeste?" Kevin shouted. "This place is awesome—how come you never had us down here before?" He slapped Travis on the back, almost sending him sprawling face-first onto the gravel driveway.

"Well, the pool's that way, but it's closed—there's a

*party* there later tonight," she said deliberately, glaring at Travis, who seemed totally oblivious. He was busy chortling at another one of his buddies, who had grabbed a hibiscus flower from a nearby bush and was prancing around with it behind his ear. "Travis," Celeste managed between clenched teeth. "Can I talk to you alone for a sec?"

"Oooh, Trav, are you in trouuubbble?" Kevin shouted as Celeste dragged her reluctant boyfriend off down the path.

Around the corner of the main building, Celeste released Travis's arm and turned to face him. "What are those guys doing here?" she hissed furiously. "I thought you were at the beach!"

Travis made little "calm down" gestures with his hands, patting the air around her like she was some hysterical child. "Look, don't freak out, okay? We *were* going to go to the beach, but then I started thinking about Nick and I thought you might need a little male protection." He winked. She remained stony-faced. "So the boys came here."

Celeste thought the top of her head was going to blow off. Her face felt tight and hot. "I honestly have no idea how you could think this would possibly be okay," she managed to say without screaming. "You know how important this is to my family. Those jerk-offs cannot come to the festival."

Travis rolled his eyes. "We were just going to hang out on the golf course anyway until the parties are over, so stop worrying."

Celeste looked at him warily. "Really?"

"Hey, baby, have I ever let you down before?" he asked, taking both her hands in his.

*Was he kidding?*

"Just keep them away, Travis," she said, pulling her arms back. "I mean it."

"Hey." He held up a Boy Scout salute. "You have my word."

Celeste eyed him for a long moment and then nodded. She spun on her heel and marched away down the path.

Back in the lobby, Celeste slipped into the ladies' room and splashed some water on her face, being careful not smudge her eye makeup. She took a few deep breaths to try to calm herself down. A toilet flushed behind her, and as she dried her hands, she could see a pair of legs dancing around in the booth. Celeste rummaged in her bag to touch up her faded lip stain and the stall door banged open. An impossibly thin woman in skin-tight gold lamé burst out.

"Ugh!" the woman exclaimed breathlessly as she turned the water taps on full force. "Why do these people have such small stalls? How do they expect anyone to do anything in there?" She had buried her ring-encrusted hands in a mound of soapsuds.

Celeste's eyes widened. She started to respond but it was obvious the woman didn't really want an answer. Celeste snuck another sidelong glance. She was probably in her midforties and had that leathery, stringy look that came with decades of diets and sunbathing. *She looks like a chicken bone.* Celeste bit the inside of her cheek to keep from laughing. But she might have let out the tiniest noise, because the woman fixed her with an intense stare in the mirror. Celeste immediately squashed all giggling and gave the woman the most sincere, polite, and demure grin she could summon. It must have done the trick, because the woman actually smiled herself and then, drying her hands on her gold jumpsuit instead of on the fluffy white towels laid out in front of her, she swept from the bathroom.

Celeste slowly followed and, nodding at the guests she passed, took up her post again at her mother's side. She spied the woman, who was now leaning over the front desk, terrorizing Michelle, the desk clerk. "Mom," she whispered. "Who is that woman?"

"That's Mila Rotterdam," her mother whispered back without changing her friendly expression.

Celeste's heart almost stopped. "Oh my God, that's *her*?" She dug in her evening bag and pulled out the little guest cheat sheet. The entry for *Rotterdams* read: *Mila and Mason. Powerful Hollywood movie producers. Dislikes:*

*Chihuahuas. Special Requests: personal trainer visit, villa 2, 7 a.m. Food: Mila, allergic to pepper.*

"There's Mason over there," Mom whispered. Celeste followed her mother's gaze across the room to a little, wizened old man who looked more like George Burns than a movie executive. He was standing in a corner, staring down at a glass of water.

"Oh," Celeste said, making a mental note to make sure Mila Rotterdam had everything her gold-laméd self desired through the course of the festival. This woman was the reason they'd had to deal with creating an hors d'oeuvres menu entirely free of pepper. Which was, it had turned out, an incredibly difficult task. Her phone beeped in her bag. She dug it out and turned away from the crowd to take a look. Text from Nick. Celeste flipped it open. SCREEN OKAY. ALL QUIET. Celeste smiled and was about to write back when her father leaned over and tapped her on the shoulder.

"Celeste, we need to start moving people into the lounge to start the cocktail party," he said sotto voce.

Celeste nodded and turned to the knot of couples standing near her. "Excuse me," she said with her best Pinyon-employee, daughter-of-the-owners smile. They looked up expectantly. "If you all would like to head into the lounge"—she pointed at the double doors— "we'll be serving drinks and appetizers shortly."

Around the lobby, the groups began breaking up and trickling slowly towards the double doors at the opposite end of the room, laughing, the women balancing on their stilettos, everyone talking excitedly. Celeste could see Mila Rotterdam clutching the arm of a guy who couldn't have been older than twenty-five and tottering toward the lounge. "... better serve some good liquor!" Celeste could hear her trumpeting. "The last place only had Wild Turkey." Celeste caught her mother's glance and discreetly rolled her eyes in the direction of Mrs. Rotterdam. Her mother sighed and nodded in agreement.

The dim, intimate lounge was perfectly laid out with sleek couches and low chairs. The soft lighting illuminated the little cocktail tables and the rich wood of the bar, but left the corners in shadows. A jazz quartet was playing in one corner. Huge potted ferns nodded their feathery heads in the corners, and votive candles flickered on the tables. Waiters in sleek black T-shirts were circulating with trays of Spanish cheeses, olives, feta dip, and lobster on water crackers.

As she looked around, Celeste felt proud. She lived at the best resort in Palm Springs. This scene belonged in a magazine. The last of the guests trickled in, and Dad shut the doors. The noise in the place swelled, and Celeste could hear laughter echoing above the conversation.

She collected a Perrier from the bar and started moving through the crowd, smiling and nodding. In the back of her mind, she wondered if Nick would change his mind and come over. "Another vodka tonic, sir?" she asked a big, red-faced man brightly. "Matthew would be happy to get you one." She indicated the waiter who had magically appeared next to her.

Just then, her father laid his hand on her shoulder. His face was calm and benign, but his eyes were sparkling dangerously. "Celeste, dear, can I speak to you for a second?" he asked quietly. *Uh-oh.* She could tell that tone immediately. It was the "you've messed up, my dear, but I don't want the guests to know there's anything wrong" tone. She knew the drill.

"Sure, Dad," she said cheerfully. Still clutching her water glass, she followed her father over to a corner partially masked by the bar.

"Celeste," her father said. "You know the next few days are some of the biggest we've ever had here at the resort, right?" His forehead looked strained.

"Yes, Dad." Celeste nodded. Did she ever.

"And that our family is going to have to work harder than ever to make sure that everything goes absolutely perfectly this weekend, right?"

"Yes, Dad," Celeste said again. She felt like a robot who'd only been programmed with one phrase.

"Then *why*," her father whispered harshly, "are those boys at this party?" He pointed. Celeste followed his hand and felt her stomach plunge into her shoes. Travis and all his buddies were coming through the doors— laughing, talking, and most definitely not sober.

# Chapter Twenty-three

✦

Celeste convulsively squeezed her Perrier glass so tightly it was a miracle it didn't shatter. What the hell were they doing? Travis had promised they'd stay away from the parties! She could hear her father breathing next to her like some sort of bull ready to stampede.

"Um, I have no idea what they're doing here, but don't worry, Dad, I'll take care of everything," she said hastily, before he could stride over there and take care of things himself. *That* could get very ugly—for Travis, at least.

"You have ten minutes, Celeste," her father said, fixing her with a piercing gaze.

"Don't worry about a thing! Look, that dude in the

feathers is asking the bartender why we don't have absinthe. You'd better go rescue him."

Her father's attention was momentarily diverted, and Celeste used the opportunity to slip over to Travis, who had flung himself on one of the sofas. His buddies had lined up at the bar, though she didn't know why they were bothering. They were obviously already drunk. Travis looked up as Celeste approached.

"Hey, babe," he said easily, reaching up to pull her into his lap. His face had that slack, red look that she knew very well signaled "Drunk Travis."

Celeste stood rigidly in front of him. "Travis," she said through her teeth. "What are you doing?"

He looked around. "Nothing much. Just hanging out. Why?"

"*Why?*" Celeste struggled to keep her voice down. "You swore you'd keep your obnoxious friends away. Now, *I'm* in deep shit—my dad is pissed beyond words." She realized she was clenching her fists so hard her fingernails were digging into her palms.

Travis looked around the room as if surprised to find himself there. "Hey, calm down," he said, reaching up for her hands. She kept them closed stiffly at her sides. "Don't get so mad. We're just hanging out. No one's doing anything," he said, shaking his head.

"I can't believe you'd just completely ignore everything I'm saying like this," she said. "Get your friends out of here, Travis—I mean it. Like now." Celeste turned and stalked away.

She wove through the crowd and went up to the bar. She leaned over the smooth dark wood. "Mike," she murmured. "Can I have a wet towel?"

The bartender looked at her with concern. "Sure, Celeste, but what's the matter? You look kind of red." He passed her a small white bar towel dampened with ice water. Celeste pressed it onto her forehead and the back of her neck.

"I'm okay, thank you. Just trying to cool down." She handed the towel back and felt a hand on her arm. She whirled around, expecting to see Travis, but instead, Nick stood behind her, wearing a slim gray suit and a big grin. "Hey," he said brightly as she stared at him. "The pool's all set up, so I decided to come over to see how everything was going." He looked around the room. "This looks awesome. Everyone looks like they're having a good time—even my mother." He pointed at Mrs. Saunders, who was in a corner stuffing feta dip into her mouth. "I need a drink—can I get a vodka and cranberry?" he asked Mike.

Celeste scanned the room rapidly. She couldn't spot Travis in the crowd, but that didn't mean he had left. She took Nick's arm and marched him away from the bar.

"Hey," Nick protested. "I was just going to get my drink—"

"Look, Travis and his friends just crashed the party," Celeste told him. "My dad's really mad, so don't make anything worse, okay?"

"Wow, okay," Nick said, looking her up and down carefully. "You look incredible, by the way."

Celeste could feel herself blush in spite of her irritation. "Thanks," she mumbled.

"Look, I'll go talk to them, okay? Maybe try to distract them or something," Nick said.

"Okay," Celeste replied doubtfully. "I'm not sure that'll work, but you can try."

"Trust me," Nick said, winking at her. He stuffed his hands in his pants pockets and strolled away.

The guys were all clustered in a corner by now, laughing hysterically about something and downing Stella Artois like it was the last beer on earth. Already some of the guests near them were turning to stare at Kevin, who was six five and topped two fifty. His face was beet red above his yellow polo shirt, and he had already spilled some beer down the front. Celeste could see her father eyeing her from across the room. She sent him a sickly smile, trying hard to ignore the sense of impending disaster that was growing like a seed in her chest.

Her mother floated by, carrying a glass of champagne and looking as if she'd never thought about a thing in her life except picking out the perfect cocktail dress. "Celeste," she murmured out of the corner of her mouth. "I've just spent the last half hour reshelving the seafood that idiot of a sous-chef left sitting out on the counter. Hopefully, we won't wind up with three hundred festival guests with food poisoning. Would you mind scanning the kitchen to make sure everything else is properly put away?"

"Sure, Mom," Celeste said, eager to escape for a minute. She pushed open the swinging doors to the little prep kitchen just off the lounge. It just had couple of stainless steel counters, an industrial microwave, a mini oven, and a big refrigerator and freezer. Someone had stuck some lettuce in the sink, where it was rapidly wilting. Celeste wrapped it up in plastic wrap and stuck it in the fridge, and then started dismantling a tower of dirty appetizer plates to be taken over to the dish room in the main kitchen later. Suddenly, over the clank of china, she heard a woman's shrieking in the next room.

*Oh no.* She wiped her hands on the front of her dress and rushed through the double doors.

The music was still playing but a group had gathered around Mila Rotterdam, who was standing up next to her seat, clutching the tablecloth. Something was wrong with her face. "I should sue every person in this place!" she was shouting. "I gave specific instructions!" Dad stood next to her, patting her arm and trying to get her to sit down. All the guests near her were whispering and talking.

*What the hell happened now?* Celeste thought as she rushed toward the group. Mr. and Mrs. Saunders stood off to one side, their faces white. Nick, Travis, and Travis's buddies were standing on the outskirts of the group, looking curious. Mila's face had an odd, lumpy appearance. Her eyes were almost squished in pockets of puffy flesh, and her lips were grotesquely swollen to twice their size, as though she'd received collagen injections that had gone very wrong.

"I gave specific instructions that no pepper was to be used in any of my food!" Mila shouted again. Her skin looked like raw meat, but her vocal cords were unaffected. Celeste's eyes flew to the salt and pepper shakers sitting in the middle of the table. Except the salt shaker was alone. She frantically scanned the area around the table and spotted the mostly empty pepper shaker laying on its side beneath the table. *Shit.*

"I have never, *never* been so poorly treated in my life!" Mila trilled at the top of her voice. She shook off Mr. Tippen's consoling hand and fished a giant burgundy handbag out from underneath the table. "Mason and I only came up here as a favor to the Saunderses. But I can see that was obviously a mistake!" she declared. "You can be sure I will never, ever be setting foot in this place again." She turned and marched toward the door.

Panic rising within her, Celeste rushed after Mila.

This was a disaster. Would the other guests follow her lead?

"Mrs. Rotterdam!" she called, hurrying after the rapidly retreating gold lamé. "Please wait!" Mila ignored her and barreled through the lobby, attracting stares from a few guests checking in at the front desk. She pushed through the glass doors to the curb. "Wait, please!" Celeste called again, wishing she'd worn lower heels. But how could she have known she'd be chasing down a swollen-faced woman in a jumpsuit tonight?

Celeste reached the curb and panted for a minute, trying to catch her breath. Mila was rummaging in her purse. "I know it's here, just a minute," she muttered to the valet.

"Um, ma'am?" Celeste tried again. Mila ignored her.

"Ah, here it is!" She held up a yellow ticket in triumph. "Villa Two. It's the white Rolls-Royce." She handed the ticket to the valet.

"No!" Celeste shouted involuntarily. Mila turned and fixed her with an icy gaze.

"So, you're going to put pepper in my food and now you're going to shout at me?" She turned away in disgust. "Let's hope the Four Seasons has rooms tonight."

Celeste lowered her voice. All her training as a Pinyon guest-soother had prepared her for this moment. "I apologize, ma'am, for my outburst and for the pepper in your food," she said sincerely. "We try to take very good care of all of our guests. Whoever is responsible for the pepper will be punished, I promise."

Mila's face still looked like it was cut from oak. Clearly, this was going take some more work. "Furthermore—"

Just then, the valet pulled up with the Rolls. Damn it, why did they always have to be so fast? He hopped out and opened the door. To Celeste's horror, Mila threw her handbag on the passenger seat and climbed in behind the wheel.

"Wait!" Celeste said hastily. Mila started to shut the door. Celeste clutched at it. "We'd like to offer you a free stay here—for as long as you like! And an upgrade—to the exclusive Desert Sun guesthouse!" Mila tugged at the door, but Celeste didn't let go.

"Let go of my door!" Mila said, still tugging.

"I-I can't!" Celeste said. *What?*

"Let go!"

"I can't! Er—my finger is stuck in the handle!" Celeste said. Quickly she jammed her hand into the door handle so hard she heard her knuckles crack. "Just give me a minute, my ring is stuck." She jiggled her hand around.

Luckily, Mila couldn't see what she was doing on the other side of the door. "You know . . ." Celeste said, as she worked her hand around. It occurred to her that she had no idea what she was going to say to this lady to get her to stay, but she just kept talking. "This festival is going to be one of the most innovative film venues in southern California—at least that's what the *Los Angeles Times* said."

"That may have been very true," Mrs. Rotterdam said, jerking at the door. "And now it will be simply that much less innovative, since my husband and I will not be attending."

"That's right!" Celeste said. *Huh?* "Er—that's also what the *Times* said."

"What?" Mrs. Rotterdam stopped tugging at the door and stared at Celeste. "What are you talking about, young lady?"

*Yeah, Celeste, what* are *you talking about?* She had no idea. She just kept babbling. "Right! The *Times* said that you and your husband would never attend such a new, fresh festival. They said you were old guard and that this stuff would be too edgy for you." Celeste gestured around Pinyon. At least Mila had stopped trying to bang her car door shut, so Celeste just took a deep breath and kept on talking. "Yeah, that's why we were so thrilled when you and Mr. Rotterdam showed up. We knew you weren't dinosaurs, like the *Times* said." Celeste pretended she didn't hear Mila's outraged squawk. "We knew you had the foresight to believe in one of the hippest new film festivals in California." She turned the full force of her intense gaze on the woman now sitting motionless behind the steering wheel.

Celeste held her breath. Then Mila's hand slowly moved to her seat belt. She unfastened it and reached for her handbag on the seat next to her. Celeste hardly dared to breathe as Mila stiffly unfolded herself from the car. She stood up and fixed Celeste with a rapier-like stare.

"I will have a double vodka tonic," she said coldly and, turning, marched back into the lobby.

"Absolutely!" Celeste said to the empty air and hurried back inside to get Mila her drink.

✦ ✦ ✦

As Celeste's heels rapidly clicked across the lobby, the door to the lounge swung open, almost smacking her in the face. Travis and his friends streamed out, all talking loudly.

"Travis!" Celeste whispered. Travis's friends kept walking.

"Celeste?" Travis said. He stopped. "What are you doing, hiding behind the door?" He gave her a charming smile, and for a brief moment Celeste almost smiled back. Then she stopped herself.

"Travis, please! I just spent the last fifteen minutes convincing Mila Rotterdam not to get in her car and drive to L.A., spreading poison about Pinyon all the way there. What was going on back there? Did you do something to her food?" She eyed him suspiciously.

"What?" Travis spread his hands. "How would I know the lady's allergic to pepper, huh?"

Celeste hesitated. The prank was so much like something he would pull, but he had a point—how *would* he have known about Mila's allergy? The VIP dossier with all that information had been on her clipboard all week, and Travis had never seen it. Besides, he'd never out-and-out lied to her before. Celeste shook her head. It couldn't have been Travis. The party was winding down. She had to just keep moving.

"Look," she said firmly. "I cannot spend this whole night trying to keep your obnoxious friends out of trouble. Get them out of here! They're all drunk. I don't want to deal with any more shit tonight, Travis— please." Celeste knew she was begging and she didn't care.

"Trav!" They both turned. Kevin gestured from the main doors. "Come on! We're going back to the golf course."

Travis turned to go and Celeste grabbed his arm. "Are you really going to just leave without saying anything to me about all this?" she asked incredulously. She couldn't believe he would act like this.

He looked down at her like he'd forgotten who she was. "Oh yeah. No, look, just stop freaking out, okay? You want to come hang out with us?"

She stared up at him in disbelief. "No, Travis, I have

to go *run a party*," she said as if talking to someone very, very slow. "I cannot go *hang out* right now."

He shrugged, totally missing the sarcasm. "Okay. See you later." He turned and headed back to where Kevin was still waiting for him. Celeste watched as they slapped hands and then pushed through the doors. All should be well now—Mila Rotterdam calmed down, Travis and the guys safely out of the way—but somehow, Celeste couldn't stuff down the sense of disaster that was swiftly growing inside her.

# Chapter Twenty-four

◆

Celeste pushed through the little gate around the deck. The pool area looked amazing. Torches flared all around the perimeter, throwing their glittering light into the perfect, still water. The lounge chairs had been removed, and easy chairs and low, padded stools had been scattered about in their place. The palm frond arches stood in different corners, with soft blue couches underneath them. At one end of the deck, the tent stood gracefully, blue and green lights strung underneath it. At the other end, the band was tuning their instruments on the stage. Sloan caught Celeste's eye as she walked past, and actually nodded. Overhead, the desert sky was sprinkled with stars, like a gorgeous velvet blanket studded with diamonds. The air was deliciously warm and soft and scented with pine carried in from the desert sands just behind the resort boundaries. Celeste spotted Nick leaning against the bar at the far end, near the huge white screen.

She went up to him. She knew she had a huge smile pasted on her face, and she didn't care. She couldn't resist doing a little ballerina twirl as she approached, making the full skirt of her silk dress flare out. He was twisting a glass beaded with moisture in one hand, but when he saw her, he quickly set it down on the wooden bar. He inhaled as she stood in front of him. There was a pause as they both looked at each other. "So, what do you think?" he asked, gesturing at the scene around him.

"It looks perfect," she said.

A big grin lit his face. He stepped forward and took her arm. "Come here. I want to show you everything." He placed her hand on the crook of his elbow as they slowly strolled along the perimeter of the pool deck. The bartender and waiters lounging against the fence looked up and smiled as they passed. The breeze lifted Celeste's hair and caressed the back of her neck. She only half listened as Nick pointed out the bar, the drinks table, the catered food laid out in long rows. She was very aware of the scratchy wool of his suit sleeve under her hand, and the warmth of his arm underneath. As he turned toward her for a second, she inhaled. Cedar. Celeste stared at Nick's face as he described dealing with the catering chef. His blue eyes, so piercing in the sunlight, looked dark and velvety in the twilight. His white teeth flashed as he spoke.

"Mmm." Celeste nodded in agreement, even though she'd heard hardly anything he'd said. She moved a step closer to him and hugged his arm a little. All of a sudden, Nick stopped talking. They locked eyes. Then, without thinking, Celeste lifted her face toward Nick's lips. He tilted his head down to hers.

Suddenly, the clash of dishes at the bar woke Celeste from her spell. She looked around. The first guests were trickling in, some still clutching glasses from the other party. Celeste and Nick could hear little "oohs" of appreciation as they took in the scene. "I can't believe it's really starting!" she whispered excitedly.

Celeste's parents came through the gate and hurried over to Celeste and Nick. The Saunderses followed close behind.

"Celeste, Nick," her father said. "This all looks fantastic. I have to say, you two really rose to the occasion." He clapped Nick on the shoulder and gave Celeste a squeeze.

"Absolutely," Mr. Saunders concurred. "Excellent work, both of you. We had wondered if giving Nick his own movie screening was the right thing to do, but after seeing how you both have pulled this together, I'm very happy we did."

Nick beamed. Guests were pouring through the gate now, laughing and talking. Sloan started the band on a fast, up-tempo song, and some people began dancing in an open space on one side of the deck.

"All right, we need to circulate," Mr. Saunders said. The four parents wandered off in different directions, all with welcoming, friendly smiles fixed on their faces.

Celeste grabbed Nick's hand. "Come on," she said. "The screening's not going to start for another half hour. Let's go sample the dessert bar before all the raspberry cheesecake is gone."

"Okay. What the–?!" Nick's reply was lost as he stumbled backwards. He made a choking sound as a hand spun him around by the collar of his shirt.

"Get your hands off my girlfriend, you piece of shit!" Travis bellowed, shoving Nick to the ground. He reeked of beer. Celeste could almost see the waves of drunkenness pouring off him. "Get up!" Nick staggered to his feet, rubbing his neck, and Travis drew his fist back to punch him.

"Travis!" Celeste screamed and grabbed his arm. He didn't even pause, just socked Nick in the jawbone. Nick staggered but didn't fall and, launching himself through the air, flung himself on Travis. Both of them fell heavily to the deck, cracking one of the teak boards under the force of their combined weight. Celeste screamed again before thinking in the back of her mind that she shouldn't be attracting more attention to the fight than it was already getting.

Nick and Travis rolled over and over on the pool deck, punching each other as hard as they could. An interested crowd was gathering around them, people still clutching drinks as if they were watching the Rumble in the Jungle. Nick managed to get on top of Travis and, straddling him, punched him hard in the face. Travis groaned and then heaved himself upright, grabbing Nick's shirt in both hands. He yelled. Celeste could see where they were heading—right for the giant white screen perched at one end of the deck. She closed her eyes and heard a crash and a whooshing noise.

When she finally dared to peek through her eyelids, the screen was gone. Only a white tangle of vinyl lay on the ground, with a large, thrashing lump underneath it. As everyone watched, the lump began moving and slowly, two heads emerged from the edge. Nick and Travis struggled to their feet. A murmur ran through the silent crowd as Celeste's father stepped forward. For a long, painful moment, he studied the two figures in front of him, Nick, dripping blood from his nose and Travis cradling his elbow. Then he turned around, and with a brilliant smile, waved his hands at the crowd.

"So sorry about this, everyone," he said calmly, his voice carrying even to the farthest gawkers on the edge of the crowed. "We were concerned you all might get bored before the screening, so we arranged this little extra—ah—*entertainment*." He smiled and everyone laughed. "Please enjoy the rest of the party."

People started turning away, talking to one another and glancing curiously at Nick and Travis, who still had not moved. Celeste's stomach was churning and her hands were icy cold. Her dad's nose was white around the edges and the back of his neck was red, but those were the only outward signs of his anger. To any other observer, he looked completely relaxed. Celeste could see the Saunderses over her father's shoulder, their faces set stonily.

Mr. Tippen turned to the group. "Why don't we all step into the office for a moment?" he said calmly. Mr. Saunders nodded his head slightly in response. The parents turned and wove their way through the crowd, with Nick, Travis, and Celeste following behind. Celeste felt like she was the one who had been in a fight. Her mind was numb, except for the vague feeling that she might throw up at any moment. Travis bumped her arm as they walked, and she jerked away. She couldn't even look at him, much less bear the thought of him touching her. Nick walked right behind. Celeste could hear his ragged breathing. She threw him a quick glance and he raised his eyes briefly to meet hers. To her shock, he winked at her. Celeste whipped her head around.

Mr. Tippen let everyone file in front of him into the

little, cramped office and then firmly shut the door. Celeste held her breath as he turned to face the assembled group: Mr. and Mrs. Saunders standing next to the desk, Celeste's mom on a straight chair, Nick slouched in the corner, and Travis on the sofa. Slowly, Mr. Tippen strode over and stood in front of Travis.

"Well, Travis," he said quietly. "You've used up your three strikes this time—and then some. Surely this was the finest display of immaturity that Pinyon has ever seen." His voice remained even, but Celeste could see his eyes flashing. Travis stared straight ahead at the wall. Celeste wasn't sure just how drunk he still was. Mr. Tippen went on. "If you haven't ruined Pinyon's first film festival, you've certainly tried your best." He paused and Celeste caught her breath. There was something about the deadly calm tone that was far worse than yelling. "Naturally, this is the last time I ever expect to see you on Pinyon premises," he said. "Please leave now."

Travis started to get up from the sofa, but before he could, Mr. Tippen turned to Celeste. Travis dropped back on the cushions as if he'd been shoved. Celeste cringed as her father's gaze fell on her with a thunk. "Celeste," he said. "You have shown spectacularly poor judgment in your constant defense of this young man in the past. At your urging, I agreed to allow him to work at Pinyon this summer and I did not fire him after his first fight with Nick here. I hold you—"

"Wait!" Nick jumped up from his chair. All heads turned toward him.

There was a moment's silence. Then Mr. Tippen said, "What is it, Nick?"

Nick looked at Celeste. "Uh, I have to make a confession." He was sitting at the very edge of the sofa, his back straight and his hands clasped between his knees.

More silence. Celeste realized she was holding her breath.

Suddenly, Nick's posture relaxed. He sprawled back against the cushions in his old cocky way and stretched his legs out in front of him. A lazy grin spread across his face. "I wouldn't be a man if I let someone else take the blame."

Mr. Tippen glanced quickly at the Saunderses. "What are you saying, Nick?" Mr. Saunders asked, his voice rising slightly.

"Dude, it wasn't Travis."

Mr. Saunders blinked.

"It was me who put the pepper in the old lady's food."

No one spoke.

"Hey, she deserved it," Nick said into the silence. "She was way too annoying."

"But why pepper, Nicky?" Mrs. Saunders whispered. Her face was white.

Nick shrugged casually. He didn't look at Celeste.

"Why not? We had all the VIP stuff written down—all the food allergies and stuff were on there."

Celeste shook her head. It didn't make any sense. Why would Nick throw away everything they'd worked on? Her brain was whirling. Then in her mind's eye, she saw Nick strolling across the room to talk with Travis and his buddies at the cocktail party. Was that what he had been doing? Plotting out a stupid, stupid, immature prank? She stared at Travis. He was sitting up in his seat, his eyes wide.

"Travis?" Celeste said weakly. He clamped his mouth shut and stared at a corner of the room. Nick watched him for a second and then went on.

"Look, I'm sorry, okay? I told Travis and the rest of the guys to try some of this wicked vodka I got from my friend, and I guess it was too much for him. The fight wouldn't have happened if it hadn't been for all that booze. I was just having some fun. So, it wasn't Travis's fault at all—or Celeste's."

Celeste could see Nick trying to catch her eye. She shot him one furious glare and then stared straight ahead.

"Oh." Mr. Tippen looked momentarily thrown off balance. He glanced at the Saunderses. It was a different situation if the son of his famous guests was causing trouble. "Er—"

Mr. Saunders stood up. He turned to Celeste's parents. "Let me apologize on behalf of my son," he said tightly. "His mother and I are shocked and ashamed." He turned to Nick. "Go home," he ordered. "The screening is canceled. Go back to the guesthouse right now. We'll discuss your punishment later."

Nick looked as if he'd been punched in the stomach all over again. The blood drained from his face. He opened his mouth but his father exploded. *"Go!"* he yelled, his composure gone. Nick scurried to the door and wrenched it open. It whooshed shut behind him.

Celeste wasn't sure if she should scream or just start crying. Nick must have done it. He must have never even cared about the screening, or he never would have risked losing everything. Her father harrumphed and cleared his throat a few times.

"Well, all right," he said. Slowly, he sank down to sit behind his desk, moving as if he were a very old man. "All right, then," he repeated. "I suppose you may go, Travis. Celeste, go with him. I, ah—well, good night." He waved his hand at them.

Out in the mostly empty lobby, Celeste turned to Travis. She was about to apologize for suspecting him of the prank and blaming him for the fight, when she saw the silly expression on his face and the glazed look in his eyes. "Travis," she said, leaning in close, "are you still drunk?"

He swayed on his feet slightly and shook his head a few times. "Hey, babe, no, I'm fine." He tried to grab her but missed and almost pitched forward onto the tile floor. Celeste just managed to catch him around the waist. Together, they staggered several steps forward and back, like the world's worst dance partners, before Travis finally got his balance.

"Oh my God," Celeste said. "Travis, get a hold of yourself. Come on." She pushed open the doors and wrangled her two-hundred-pound boyfriend out onto the path. She draped his arm over her shoulder and steered him toward the staff quarters. She could hear the remnants of the ruined party in the background. Travis almost took several dives into the bushes at the side of the paths, but after a few tense minutes, they made it to her parents' bungalow. "Here," Celeste panted, unlocking the door and shoving Travis inside. "You can sleep in my room tonight. Mom and Dad won't be back until late."

"Yeah!" Travis mumbled, his eyes already drooping. He swiped at her. "Sounds good, babe. . . ." His voice trailed off and his knees buckled. Celeste grabbed him again.

"Travis! Do not go to sleep right here. You have to get down the hall."

Travis headed straight for the bed once in Celeste's room. Still wearing his shoes, he collapsed on the flowered comforter and immediately fell asleep. Celeste flicked on the bedside lamp and stood staring at him for a long time. He was lying on his back, and his lips flapped like two sausages as he snored. He smelled of sweat and stale liquor.

Finally, Celeste turned the light off and went into the bathroom. The bright yellow light of the little room seemed calm and sane after the craziness of the evening. All her bottles and jars were neat and straight on the clean counter, and her own fluffy towels hung on the towel rack. She turned on the taps of the bathtub full blast and dumped in some bath powder. Fragrant, foamy water started rising in the tub.

She stripped off the creased, sweaty silk dress and climbed into the warm water. She lay back and spread a washcloth over her eyes. Maybe if she just relaxed, she wouldn't have to face the fact that she had trusted Nick and he had completely betrayed her. She clenched her fists on the side of the tub as this thought flooded over her and shook her head. How could he have done this?

She cringed as she thought of everything she'd told Nick about her writing, and the resort, and her parents. She'd thought that he was more than just an arrogant pretty boy, but obviously she should have trusted her first instincts. All he cared about was amusing himself and making trouble between her and Travis. Celeste closed her eyes and let the warm bathwater lap over her body. The festival had just begun, but it didn't matter. Her summer was already over.

# Chapter Twenty-five

✦

The rest of the festival was uneventful. Celeste played the role of owners' daughter perfectly, seeing to guest requests and smiling politely for hours at a time. She hadn't seen Travis since leaving him to sleep off his hangover in her bed while she returned to work four days ago. She assumed Nick was under house arrest in his parents' villa, since she hadn't seen him since he left her father's office. Despite not having to face him, she hadn't been able to shake a near-constant headache.

The day after the festival's closing party, Celeste woke up at ten. Her head was pounding and the sight of her crumpled pink silk dress still sitting in the corner of her room didn't help. Devon's plane was set to arrive at eleven. Celeste briefly considered texting and telling her to get a cab. She didn't really feel like talking to anyone. But maybe a ride to the airport would clear her head. Celeste rolled off the bed and threw on the first jeans and T-shirt her hand touched.

Outside, the light morning breeze played over her skin and the sun was touching the red azaleas lining the path. Celeste glanced at her watch and walked a little faster. Suddenly, she bumped straight into Nick, who was struggling down the path, laden with two big suitcases.

Celeste gasped in surprise and jumped back. Nick stopped short. His face was creased and puffy. "You look terrible," Celeste said involuntarily.

"My parents are sending me back to L.A.," he said woodenly. "The car's waiting for me."

Celeste felt anger boiling up inside her. "Good," she said harshly. Nick winced. Celeste brushed past him. She could feel his forlorn gaze between her shoulder blades but she refused to turn around. She had no desire to waste one more second on someone who had played her all summer and then wasted her time and hard work on something he'd never cared about anyway.

At the airport, Celeste stood on her tiptoes, trying to see past the crowd waiting by the baggage claim. A lot of people were coming up the escalator, but there was still no sign of Devon. It seemed like two years since she'd left, instead of a few weeks. Suddenly, she heard her name.

"Celeste!" Devon yelled, and flung her arms around her friend.

"Oh my God! I can't believe you're back!" Celeste said. "I missed you." Devon was wearing a tank top with the Scottish flag on it tucked into skintight black jeans, and stiletto ankle boots. "You look like a member of the Clash."

"I can't believe I'm back either," Devon replied, turning to survey the baggage carousel, now jammed with luggage. "I need a Diet Coke, like, right now. Scotland is amazing, but they're way too into tea. Hey, there's mine!" She muscled her way through the crowd and snared an enormous black duffel bag.

"So," Devon said a few minutes later, as the girls wound their way through a concrete maze of sidewalks and blast barriers on their way to the parking garage. "I'm dying to know how the film festival went. Did you meet any celebrities?" She cast a sideways glance at Celeste.

"Oh, um, I can't remember." Celeste managed to avoid looking at her friend by scanning the aisles of parked cars. "So, uh, what was the food like there?"

"Celeste! What is going on? I can tell something's up," Devon said. She tossed her bag into the backseat of the Civic before climbing into the front and settling back on the cracked leather. Celeste got in and slammed the door. She turned the ignition and then sat for a minute, her hand on the gearshift, staring through the windshield. Devon tactfully gazed out the window at the side of the car parked next to them. Then Celeste threw the car into reverse and started maneuvering out of the parking space. She heaved a giant sigh. "You know, the whole thing makes me want to puke when I even think about it, Dev," she said.

"What? What happened? You're driving me crazy with all of this drama." Devon waved her arms around her head.

"It was a complete failure," Celeste said, looking over her shoulder to merge onto the highway. Briefly, she filled Devon on the party details, the Rotterdam pepper prank, and the Nick-Travis blowout at the screening party. "And so his parents canceled his screening and are sending him back to L.A.," she finished.

"Wow." Devon let out her breath in a deep exhale. "So he totally confessed, huh? Like said he did it right out?"

"Well, yeah! I was sitting right there," Celeste exclaimed. The car's speedometer crept up to seventy.

"Okay, don't kill us," Devon said, eyeing the dashboard. "I'm just really surprised Nick would do something like that."

Celeste snorted. "I'm not," she said shortly. "I was

such an idiot to think he actually cared about the screening and the resort. It turned out that all he cared about was screwing with me and trying to destroy my relationship, for his own sick fun."

"Yeah . . ." Devon replied slowly. "I guess so." She fell silent and drummed her Chanel Vamp–painted nails on the window. Celeste slowed down and stared straight ahead at the clogged highway in front of her. Devon fidgeted with the strap on her bag. She crossed and uncrossed her legs. Finally, Celeste couldn't stand it anymore.

"Devon!" she burst out. "What is it? You're driving me crazy. What? Did you bring home some secret husband from Scotland or something?"

Her friend forced a laugh. "Uh, yeah, very funny." She cleared her throat. "I, uh, well, I'm just really surprised that Nick would do that at the party, because he was really crushing on you all summer."

Celeste looked over at her friend. Devon was staring at her lap.

"I mean, all that time Nick and I were hanging out, before I left, all he ever did was talk about you," she said. "I tried to hook up with him a bunch of times, but he just wasn't interested. I didn't tell you because I thought you'd be annoyed that he was all hung up on you. I mean, you had Travis." She glanced at Celeste nervously. "It was weird. . . . I felt like I was cheating with him or something."

"No! Of course you weren't," Celeste said automatically. Nick was hung up on her . . . but he'd ruined the party. And he'd gotten Travis drunk just to make trouble. Celeste shook her head. "He was probably just saying all that to mess with your mind," she told Devon.

"Maybe," Devon said doubtfully. She was quiet for a minute. "So, is everything cool with you and Travis now?"

"Mostly." Celeste shrugged as she pulled into Devon's driveway. "Honestly, I've barely seen him since the whole mess at the festival. Just a couple of texts. We're still driving to Tempe tomorrow though. Maybe we just need some time alone together. By the way, he and the guys are having a barbecue over at Kevin's later. You want to go over with me?"

"Sure! Let me jump in the shower."

When the girls arrived several hours later, the guys were already ensconced on the back deck. The sun was just going down over the desert horizon. Kevin was anxiously hovering over some hamburger patties and skewers of onion and peppers sizzling on a DCS Professional grill, which stretched almost the entire back length of the deck. The rest of the guys were immersed in what looked like an intense game of water polo in the pool. As Celeste and Devon approached, Travis scored a goal and let out a wild yell of triumph, raising both fists in the air.

"Hey, guys!" Devon caroled. Everyone looked up.

"Hey there," Travis greeted them, his eyes on Celeste.

She gave him a small smile but couldn't muster up more than that. She was starting to feel tired of the guys. *You just need to get away*, she told herself. *You've been trapped here all summer.*

The girls dropped their bags on one of the deck chairs and stripped off their sundresses. Celeste adjusted her black bikini top and climbed onto another chair. She sighed and lay back. The evening sun felt wonderful. Then a shadow blocked the sunlight and cold drips of water fell on her bare stomach. She opened her eyes. Travis was standing over her, panting and grinning. All of other guys had climbed from the pool too and were wiping themselves with towels and digging around in the little portable fridge on the deck for beers.

"So, what's up with you, Devon?" Brent asked, emptying half his beer at one gulp. "Weren't you in Ireland or something?"

"Scotland," Devon corrected. "It was awesome. I missed home though."

"Well, don't worry. You didn't miss anything here," Brent said. "This summer has been completely lame as far as excitement."

"Oh, I don't know," Kevin said lazily, leaning his head back and draining his beer. "We had some pretty good fun at the resort the other night."

Celeste lifted her head. Fun? What was he talking about?

Kevin chortled. "I can't believe that rich little prick took all the blame." He got up to dig for another beer. Celeste froze. She heard Travis's breath catch, but her eyes refused to focus on anything.

"Yeah, that was crazy," Brent agreed. "But hell, if he wanted to say he did it, I've got no problem with Travis keeping his mouth shut."

Celeste sat straight up in her chair. She grabbed the sides with both hands, almost scorching her palms on the hot metal. All the guys turned toward her. Devon was also sitting up, her eyes wide as she stared at her friend.

Celeste tried to control her pounding heart. "Hey, Travis," she said in a horrible approximation of nonchalance. "Um, I'm feeling kind of slow right now. What are they talking about?"

Travis shot a warning look at his buddies. "Nothing, babe."

Kevin was leaning over the beer cooler and didn't catch Travis's glare. "It's just weird that dude Nick said that he put the pepper in the old lady's food."

"Why was it weird?" Celeste asked in a strangled voice.

Travis looked at her warily.

Celeste shot up from her chair, knocking it sideways onto the deck. "*You* did it!" she screeched, pointing at Travis. Brett sat motionless and Kevin's mouth dropped open. "You did it! You put the pepper in Mila's food! You—"

Her words were cut off as a pair of slim arms wrapped around her waist.

"Sorry, guys! Phew! It's hot out here. Celeste, let's get some ice," Devon caroled as she half carried, half dragged Celeste through the sliding glass doors and into the kitchen.

Once inside, she deposited Celeste in a heap on the floor and pulled the doors shut behind them. She snapped the blind down as Travis's anxious face appeared at the window and knelt beside her friend. Celeste lay curled up on the linoleum.

Devon stroked her hair back from her forehead. "Travis pulled the prank," Celeste finally said in a muffled voice.

"Yeah."

"Travis screwed up the whole evening."

"It looks that way." Devon got up and ran a glass of water. She sat back down on the floor. Celeste sat up and took a sip.

"Then Nick . . ."

"Yeah?" Devon said encouragingly.

"Nick . . . didn't do it. Then why did he say he did?" Celeste's mouth felt very slow.

"Celeste." Devon propped her friend up against the cabinets. "You're being very dense, chick. Nick was trying to bail you out! He knew that your dad would be furious if he thought it was Travis who pulled all that stuff. So he just took the blame."

Celeste shook her head. "But Nick got in all sorts of trouble. Why would he do that to himself if he didn't do anything?"

Devon grabbed Celeste by the upper arms and shook her. "Has the sun fried your brain? He was trying to keep you from getting in trouble! He was, like—sacrificing himself."

"Whoa," Celeste said slowly. "And Travis—"

"Just sat there and let him do it," Devon finished.

"Oh my God," Celeste said. "Oh my God! But this whole time I thought he was just playing around, trying to make trouble because he was bored."

"Guess you were wrong, huh?" Devon stood and then reached down and pulled her friend up. "We can't stay in here sitting on the floor forever. Are you ready to go out and drown Travis in the pool? I'll help you if you want."

"Thanks for the offer." Celeste stood thinking for a moment. She turned toward the kitchen and then turned back. "No, I'll call Nick first. Then I'll kill Travis."

"Celeste, don't be such an idiot!" Devon practically shouted. "The guy just totally martyred himself for you and you're going to *call* him? Go find him!"

"Drive to L.A.? Now? But it's seven o'clock! And I'm

supposed to go to Tempe tomorr—wait a minute." Celeste realized what she was saying. "I'm *not* going to Tempe tomorrow."

Devon just stood, watching her friend.

"I think I'm going to L.A.," Celeste said.

"Woo-hoo!" Devon flung her arms into the air. "You rock, girl. Don't waste one more second on Travis the Asshole."

Celeste hugged Devon as hard as she could. Then she walked out the door, leaving Devon standing in the hall behind her, the world's biggest grin on her lips. As she ran down the walk to the Civic, Celeste's plan fell into place in her mind, like coins clinking into a row of slots. She glanced at her watch. If traffic was on her side, she could be in L.A. by eleven o'clock. She only hoped she wasn't too late.

# Chapter Twenty-six

◆

Celeste pulled away from the curb, her headlights cutting a long white beam into the descending desert evening. She had to find Nick. She had to tell him—what? That she was sorry, first of all. And . . . she'd figure the rest out later. Maybe she'd know what to say when she saw him. But she had to see him.

Back at the resort, Celeste let herself into the quiet office. She flicked on one of the computers. While it booted up, she stared into the falling shadows, thinking of Nick's face that morning. His blue eyes had been so sad. The computer beeped and she quickly drew up the master guest list. Sanderson, Sanstein, Saunders. Thirty-two Waterwood Court. She plugged the address into

Google, grabbed the directions from the printer, and turned off the computer.

As she got up to leave, she heard the office door open behind her.

"Celeste . . ." Travis's voice was pleading as she turned to face him. "I–"

"Stop." She cut him off. Storming past him into the darkened lobby, Celeste realized that she had to deal with this. Taking a deep breath, she tried to keep her anger from boiling over.

Seizing on her pause, Travis stepped forward and put his hand on the small of her back. "Celeste, I'm so–"

"No, Travis. You don't get to talk." Celeste spun around to face him. "You don't get to try to make this better. Because this isn't about the prank. Or even about letting Nick, who happens to be the son of my parents' very best clients, take the fall for you." She could feel her momentum building. Travis dropped his hand to his side and Celeste stood up straighter.

"This is about me, and my family, and our business. You knew exactly how important this festival was to us. But, just like you did all summer, you completely disregarded my feelings. I begged you–begged–to leave Nick alone, to give me a break, to trust me and let me do what was best for my family. And you ignored every word. I can't be with someone like that. So don't apologize. Just go."

Travis's jaw had dropped slightly, but he closed his mouth and collected himself. "Look, I'm sorry I got so jealous. I just couldn't stand the way he looked at you all the time. It made me crazy."

Celeste laughed. "Wow. Again, my very simple request gets ignored. I understand being jealous once, but after I assured you that it was *you* I wanted to be with? That's called trusting your girlfriend, Travis. And maybe not doing exactly what you felt like doing exactly when you felt like doing it. For once. So how about, for the first time in our relationship, you just listen to me? Please. Leave."

Travis didn't move. Rather than waste another moment, she walked past him to the door leading outside. Pushing it open, she paused and turned her head back.

"Just so we're clear, Travis," she said calmly. "We're very, very over. Good luck in college." With that, she stepped into the desert night.

Once she was back in the car, Celeste floored the accelerator. Now that she knew the truth, she couldn't stand to let Nick think she blamed him. And Travis . . . Celeste shook her head. She'd figure out what to do about him later. Right now, she needed to focus on Nick.

The two-hour drive to the coast seemed like ten. Even though she drove seventy the whole way, Celeste felt like the exits were creeping by. Finally, the orange night glow of L.A. shone ahead of her, like some sort of apocalypse on the horizon. She slowed down as the suburbs started flashing by and consulted her directions. Right on Route 25. Straight for five miles, then left on Wilton Boulevard. Celeste peered through the windshield. The street sign for Waterwood loomed on her right. She turned. Her heart was pounding and her hands were sweaty on the steering wheel.

Nick's house—or mansion, Celeste noted—stood at the top of a little hill, the broad green lawn sweeping up to wide terrace in front, circled by the smoothly paved driveway. The black Mercedes was parked in the driveway. The house windows were dark. Celeste parked at the curb and cut the motor. She could feel the adrenaline that had fueled her through the ride slowly evaporating. What was she going to do now—ring the doorbell and explain to Mr. Saunders why she was showing up at his house at almost midnight, wearing nothing but a sundress and a black bikini? Somehow, she didn't think that would go over too well. Just then, the sweep of headlights across her windshield almost blinded her. A car was turning up the Saunderses' driveway. Celeste leaned forward, alert again. In the reflection from the porch light, she could see it was the Alfa Romeo. As she watched, the headlights went off and a moment later, a lean, shadowy figure emerged.

Celeste leaped from the Civic. "Nick!" she shoutwhispered across the lawn. He didn't hear her. He pocketed a set of keys and started toward the front door.

Celeste sprinted across the grass. "Nick!" she whispered again. This time, he turned around.

"Celeste?" he said. She ran up, tripping and almost falling against him. He caught her by the arms. "What are you doing here?" His blond hair shone under in the dim light and his eyes were deep in their sockets. His cheekbones stood out sharply in his tanned face.

Celeste's breath caught as she looked at him. "I know you didn't do it," she whispered.

He released her arms. "What are you talking about?"

"The festival! I know you didn't pull the prank or get Travis drunk." The words tumbled out of her mouth, almost falling over each other.

Nick stared at her, a flush rising in his cheeks. "You know?"

"That's why I drove all the way out tonight. I had to tell you that . . ." Celeste paused. His gaze was locked onto hers. "That I'm sorry about everything. I didn't know. I thought you were just trying to get in between me and Travis."

Nick shook his head. "I just couldn't stand seeing you get in trouble because of that jerk–" He stopped suddenly and bit his lip.

Celeste reached out and touched his hand. "Look, I'm so sorry that my stupid boyf–" She caught herself. "*Ex*-boyfriend cost you your big break." She broke off. Nick was leaning toward her intensely. "What?"

He shook his head as if to clear it. "I'm sorry—did you say *ex-boyfriend*?"

Celeste thought a minute. "Yeah, I did," she said slowly. "Travis is now officially my ex. I do kind of regret not getting to slam a door in his face or anything. Maybe I can work that in at some point."

"That's a good idea," Nick said softly. His gaze was too intense. Celeste tried to look away, but he caught her chin gently in his hand. "I'm glad you're here. We can . . . go somewhere." He gestured at the dark, empty street and Celeste giggled in spite of herself. Nick smiled ruefully. "Okay, well, maybe in the morning we can go some-where." He slid his hands up the backs of her arms and she shivered a little. "Cold?" he asked, his breath on her cheek.

Celeste shook her head. She didn't trust herself to say anything. She kept her eyes on Nick's as he pulled her against him and lowered his head. His lips were warm and firm when he kissed her. She drew back after a long moment.

"I think you've gotten better at this since last sum-mer," she teased. He grinned and wrapped his arms around her waist tightly. He pulled her in close. She could feel the muscles of his chest pressing against her.

"Well, I've been practicing," he told her, flashing the old Nick grin.

"Hey!" She punched him lightly on the arm.

"All because I was waiting for you," he amended, the

grin still lingering around the corners of his mouth. He kissed her again, long and firm.

Celeste didn't know how long they stood together under the porch light, their arms entwined around each other, his blond head bent over hers, but it felt like they were making up for lost time—a whole summer's worth.

What if your summer fling turns out to be your dream guy? Read on for a sneak peek at Hailey Abbott's

# BOY CRAZY

I declare this a ten-boy summer!"

Greta Crocker's voice rang through the bedroom, distracting Cassie Morgan from the late afternoon view of the Hollywood Hills, complete with Hollywood sign. The vista over her parents' backyard and across her posh Hancock Park neighborhood reminded her that she was finally back where she belonged. Home—where Siskiyou Academy gossip, especially the Cassie-specific item involving Daniel Fletcher and her broken heart, couldn't touch her.

Cassie fiercely tried to shake off thoughts of him as he'd shaken her off because he "needed his space." *It's summer. No ex-boyfriends or boarding school drama allowed.*

"What do ten boys have to do with our reunion summer?" Cassie made a face at her oldest friend. Greta was stretched out across Cassie's four-poster bed as if it was her own—as if it had been moments rather than months since she and Cassie had laid eyes on each other.

"It's time to take our game to the next level before senior year starts," Greta said firmly. "Hence, ten boys."

"I was thinking more like the no-boys level," Cassie suggested, leaning back against the windowsill and smiling. "I'm ready to declare myself a boy-free zone after this last year. At least for a little while."

"Agreed." Keagan Ellison wrinkled up her perfect little nose and looked up from the thick blue carpet. She lay on her stomach, kicking her long, tanned legs up behind her. Cassie's father would have a heart attack if she tried to wear anything as short as Keagan's tiny white jean cutoffs.

"I'm still recovering from the Zachary Malone disaster," Keagan said. She shuddered dramatically, making her high, pale blond ponytail bounce. "Ugh."

"Zachary Malone is a loser, not a disaster," Greta said, rolling her eyes.

"What about you, Cassie?" Keagan asked, after sticking her tongue out at Greta. "How did your heart get broken? Vicious other woman?"

Cassie sank down on to the plush carpet and flexed

her toes so she could see the bright pink pedicure she'd given herself peeking out from the ragged hem of her much-abused Lucky jeans.

"We were together all year. Then right before he left for his summer trip to Europe—with about seventeen girls, by the way—he suddenly needed space."

"Jerk!" Keagan said with feeling.

"I think you guys need to seriously consider my plan," Greta continued. "My philosophy is that dating like guys is the only way to have fun with the whole process. Because what happens if you date like a girl? You get played like a girl. And meanwhile, he's off scampering around Europe with a posse of available women."

"Ouch," Cassie said, only half kidding. Keagan raised her eyebrows in agreement.

"So why can't we do the playing?" Greta continued. "That's the beauty of the ten-boy summer. We'll have an agreement—a quota that must be reached. You have to make it to ten, so you can't get too close to any one guy."

"What if you want to get close?" Keagan asked.

"You don't," Greta retorted. "Getting close is what made you cry in the first place. Why would you want to repeat the Zachary experience?"

Cassie grinned into the darkness. "Am I crazy?" she asked Keagan. "Or is she making sense?"

"It's the wave of the future!" Greta cried. "Come on,

ladies—this calls for an official pledge." She placed her right hand over her heart and held her left hand in the air. "I, Greta Crocker, do solemnly swear that I will kiss *at least* ten boys this summer, so help me God." She finished and raised her eyebrows at the other two, issuing her challenge.

Keagan laughed again. "Okay, okay," she said. "I give in." She assumed the position. "I, Keagan Ellison, do solemnly swear that I will kiss ten boys this summer and forget all about Zachary Malone, that evil loser." She shrugged. "So help me God."

"You're up, Cassie," Greta said, eyeing her. "Or are you going to sit around and *observe* all summer?"

Cassie sighed, pretending to be put out.

"I *guess* I can try to kiss some hot guys," she said, pursing her lips as if it required an internal battle. "I mean, it's gonna be a struggle."

"Poor baby," Greta teased.

"I, Cassie Morgan, do solemnly swear that I will kiss ten extremely cute boys this summer," Cassie intoned, her left hand in the air and the other tight against her chest. "I swear that I will have fun, as ordered by Greta. So help me God."

"Bring it on!" Greta cried.

"Watch out, L.A.!" Keagan called, and then collapsed into giggles.

"Let the ten-boy summer begin," Cassie pronounced,

feeling the magic of summer spool out before her, drawing her in.

"So," she said seriously, eyeing the other two. "Does anyone know where Robert Pattinson hangs out? Because I think we should start there."

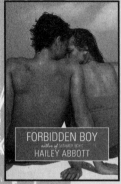
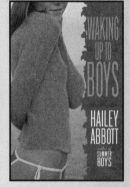

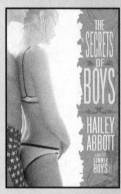

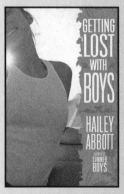